new century
PUBLISHING

KRISTIN LEE

HERRMANN

For
Darrin, Rachel, & Rylee -
With Much Love
Kristin

CIRCLES AND STANZAS

NEW CENTURY PUBLISHING

Printed in the United States of America

Library of Congress Cataloging-in-Publication Data
Herrmann, Kristin Lee
Circles and Stanzas
by Kristin Lee Herrmann

ISBN 978-0-9822344-7-1

1040 E. 86th Street, Suite 42A
Indianapolis, IN 46240

Dedication

for my mother

special thanks to Dedaimia, Mel, Lori, St,
Becca, Vickie, Catherine, and Julie

love to Cassie, Judy, Jodi, Shannon, Matt, Jim,
Wilburn, Doug, Andrew, John and
Charles, who drew lines instead of circles

Chapter One

Annie sat in the sun on the concrete steps, looking out over the river. She sat with her journal open on her lap, her pencil sharpened. She waited with eager anticipation to receive words for a new poem. Behind and above her on the playground, she heard children laughing as they pumped their legs on the swings and slid, one at a time, down the straight metal slide. Below her on the parking lot, she saw two shiny pick-up trucks hitched to empty speedboat trailers, still wet from being backed into the river. A breeze blew off the river, cooling Annie from the summer sun and tickling the tips of her toes.

Taking deep breaths, Annie tried to ignore the twinge of excitement she felt. She was about to receive the beginning of a new poem. *Patience*, she commanded. She sat with her pencil poised on the journal's page. From her daily routine of walking to the dock and sitting on the steps to write, she knew the words never came on demand. They came only as a gift…wonderful and fantastic, greater than all Christmas and birthday presents combined. Yet she didn't know from where it came.

The gift first presented itself two years ago, during the summer before Annie's freshman year of high school. It was the summer Grandma Jo passed away, causing Annie and Mother to move from Grandma Jo's house in the country into their run-down apartment in the center of the small town. At the time of the move, neither of them cared much about the apartment building's chipped paint and missing-bricks exterior. "We're not trying to impress anyone," they agreed. "It'll only be temporary," Mother stated, as they stared at the stained kitchen counter, discolored bathroom sink, and soiled carpet. Annie agreed, knowing it was their only option for the small amount of money Mother had in her purse.

Not long after moving in, Annie took off on foot to explore the small river town. She began by walking to the high school, wanting to know how long she could sleep in now that she didn't have to stand alone in the dark sky of early morning waiting for the school bus to rattle down the gravel road. From the school she walked to the town's pizza parlor, where she bought a gumball with the quarter she found at the curb in the parking lot. She savored the gum, knowing it was a poor substitute for a triangle-piece of pizza topped with melted mozzarella cheese. After the flavor was all gone, she spit the gum out and walked down the street to the river dock. The town was so tiny its residents always referred to the small landing area as the dock.

She was leaning against the stone wall which separated the playground from the street, watching a barge loaded with coal drift by, when the first line of a poem formed in her head. It was an odd line and it didn't mean anything to her, yet she couldn't forget it. She was already in bed that night when, in the dark, she scribbled it down on a tissue from the box on her nightstand. The next morning she copied it onto a piece of paper and returned to the dock. As she sat on a playground swing watching a family put their boat in the river, the second line of the poem formed in her mind. This time, knowing something special was happening, she copied the line to the paper as soon as she returned home.

Wanting to know the next lines of the poem, she began to wake herself hours before the start of her work shift as a cashier at the small grocery store located up the street from their apartment. Still wiping the sleep from her eyes, Annie walked to the edge of town to sit on the steps between the dock and the playground. There she sat with the journal she'd found in the school supplies aisle at the grocery store and purchased with part of her first paycheck. There she waited for and embraced the next stanzas, lines, or words of the poems unfolding before her. There were periods of time when she waited for weeks to receive the words which seemed to be carried to her by the wind. Annie learned to appreciate the words, presented only when the giver wanted.

It was on her way home from one such fruitless morning, two years ago, Annie met her neighbor Kelly Foster. Kelly spotted Annie and called out to her. Kelly sat on the white bench swing hanging on the front porch of her beautiful, large two-story yellow-sided house, painting her toenails a deep, rich red. It was a shade Annie found too bold for Kelly's pale skin, yet she'd never think of telling Kelly that. As Kelly finished painting her last nail, Annie looked at Kelly's blond curled hair clipped back from her face and then observed her own long, brown limp hair in the window's reflection.

They established Annie was new in town and they would both be freshmen in the fall. Pleased to have found a new friend, Annie spent her evenings after work helping Kelly with small chores Kelly's mother was unable to do because of some permanent injuries she'd suffered in a car accident. It was on one such evening, as they pulled weeds from the flowerbeds, Annie shared her gift theory regarding her poems and speculated on its unknown source. At once Kelly requested

Annie recite something she'd written. After doing so, Kelly became "convinced" of Annie's talent and declared the "gift" could only be from God.

"It's blasphemous to think it comes from anyone else," Kelly declaired as she repositioned herself to let a young couple pushing a stroller pass on the sidewalk. Annie followed Kelly's lead and scooted aside.

Kelly continued, "Who else besides God is able to create something out of nothing?"

"I guess…I thought…maybe…a relative or guardian angel or something," Annie replied, wanting to be honest but fearing she'd sound blasphemous. She wondered if the source of the gift might be Grandma Jo, who had taken her and Mother in after Father left and Mother lost her job.

Moving in with Grandma Jo had meant moving from the big city to the country outskirts of the small river town Annie now called home. There were only two stoplights and no fast food restaurants. At the time of the move, Annie was so young she threw a tantrum when she learned she wouldn't get any more kids' meal toys. But then she learned Grandma Jo had a sweet tooth for name brand, sugary cereals always containing a toy in the box and was fine with the move. Of course, now she was older Annie knew Grandma Jo's satisfied sweet tooth hurt her diabetes, and at night when Annie lay in bed missing her grandmother's boisterous laughter, she wished she hadn't taken such delight in those stupid toys.

"Annie, guardian angels protect you. They don't give you things. You have to pray to God for what you want, and so it is God who you need to thank." Kelly pushed her curly blond hair out of her face and tossed a weed into the grassy patch between the sidewalk and the street.

Annie concentrated hard on pulling a stubborn weed. "I'm not sure if that makes sense," Annie replied. "I mean, I've been given some really good poems." She didn't want to brag, but she was thinking about the winning poem she entered in the library's contest which would be published in the local newspaper the next week. "But I haven't been praying."

"You haven't been praying?" Kelly exclaimed. She shifted her gaze from the flower beds to look across the street at the apartment complex where Annie lived. With the sun setting, the building looked neglected and gloomy. The window trim, once painted a brilliant white, was noticeably dirty, peeling, and missing under some windows. The concrete retaining wall running along the sidewalk needed to be patched, and the small grass yard was full of weeds and rocks from the parking lot needing to be repaved.

Kelly nodded as though she remembered not to expect great things from someone who lived in a place that "devalued her own house," as her dad often commented. In contrast, there were no obstructions keeping the setting sunlight from blessing the full front of Kelly's house. Kelly's house was immaculate. (Annie noticed Kelly's dad washing it with a garden hose when she left for work that morning.) The bushes lining the yard were manicured into even squares. Annie couldn't recall a time when Kelly's house didn't look perfect-her house never looked gloomy.

Annie heard the familiar tone in Kelly's voice indicating Kelly was about to teach Annie something Kelly assumed Annie didn't know. Kelly took this tone when she tried to make Annie's life "easier," for example, by persuading her to wear trendier clothes and make-up.

"Annie, if nothing else, put on something to cover up the pimples on your forehead," she'd begged.

Annie ignored the lectures, having more important things to worry about, such as helping Mother pay the rent. Annie preferred having skin spotted with blemishes to being homeless. Or at least that's what she told herself when the acne creams she bought at the grocery store didn't work.

"Annie, you should pray to God every day. The only way to get into Heaven is through Him. You never know when your time will come, so you should be ready to go at any time. I like you. I'd hate to think you wouldn't make it into Heaven." Kelly paused, surprising Annie with an opportunity to respond. Annie furrowed her brow as if deep in thought. She pushed aside some mulch to grab a weed at its base. She felt Kelly watching her.

"Would you like to come to church with us sometime?" Kelly asked.

Annie didn't have to fake a look of surprise. The invitation directly violated their unspoken rule. Kelly and Annie were to be friends only when the two of them were both alone. In Annie's mind, Kelly had been the one to set the rule on their first day of high school. Annie had waved to her in the hall before second period when Kelly walked by with her friends. It'd been obvious Kelly was part of the popular crowd, and Annie contemplated not waving, yet she had, and in response Kelly looked away and started talking to the boy on her right. She acted as though she didn't know Annie had waved, never mind having spent many summer evenings talking with her!

Of course, Annie's feelings were hurt. She hurried into the closest bathroom and stood in front of the mirror, washing her hands. As she scrubbed them with liquid soap, she dared herself to cry. After that, Annie made up her mind to never acknowledge Kelly at school, which was fairly easy because they didn't share any classes or friends. Annie contemplated never speaking to Kelly again, but by the next time they ran into each other outside their homes, enough time had passed for Annie's feelings to no longer be hurt. *There are more important things than having Kelly Foster as a friend*, Annie convinced herself as she sat down on Kelly's porch swing to talk. Over time, Annie grew to appreciate the rule. It was nice to be able to talk to someone without the pressures of a public friendship.

Still, not wanting to be blasphemous, she accepted Kelly's invitation to attend church. But she accepted with hesitation. She knew Kelly's congregation was considered by some in town to be a bit odd, like a cult, even though it was a Christian denomination. The cult reference began years ago when the church hailed Kelly's mom as a miracle, resulting from their worship, because she'd survived the car accident. They celebrated their answered prayers by standing in a circle in a field beside the sanctuary, singing hymns. (Knowing Kelly's mom's injuries still affected her, for instance keeping her from sitting on the ground to pull weeds from her flower beds, Annie wondered why, if the church had such power, it didn't focus more of its worship on eliminating her pain.)

Annie didn't put much stock in the cult reference, even though it was odd the time members carried their Bibles in front of them as they walked around town in response to the video store starting a "mature adult" movie section. From behind her own Good Book, Kelly explained how its presence kept the devil from capturing their souls as he had the movie store's owner. Annie wanted to ask how the devil could be so strong when their faith was so great, but she remained quiet.

"Oh," Annie said, wiping the beads of sweat off her forehead and tossing another weed to the side, "I work on the weekend. When does your church meet?"

"Sunday mornings at 11:00."

With a bit of excitement, Annie responded, "Right now I work during that time. Can I get back to you if my hours change?"

"Sure," Kelly replied. Both girls continued to pull weeds. Annie relished in the relief she felt and assumed Kelly did, too.

After a period of silence, Kelly continued, "You really should pray. At least thank God for the gift you have."

Annie nodded, though she wasn't sure if she even knew how to pray. She'd heard televangelists use phrases like "We lift up to You" and "In the name of Your Son." But even with her gift of words, she wasn't ever able to assemble a prayer like the ones she heard on the television. She'd tried once, before a huge world history exam covering five chapters. She was about as successful speaking the prayer as she was passing the test.

"And you should probably confess your sins while you're at it," Kelly added, starting to stand up since they'd reached the end of the long flowerbed.

Annie didn't take Kelly's advisement, like her other lectures, to heart in the way Kelly desired. But Annie did walk away determined to be more thankful for the gift of words. It was a determination she brought with her to the dock each day, that day included. Annie noticed the sun had already dried one of the empty boat trailers and heard the daycare teachers blowing their whistles to assemble the group of children on the playground. As Annie sat on the concrete steps overlooking the river, she raised her head and felt the warm breeze brush against her make-up-free cheeks. She took another deep breath and gave silent thanks. Then she lowered her head and began to write.

Chapter Two

Today's gift consisted of the first few lines of a new poem. Annie was grateful. She placed her pencil in her journal and wrapped her arms around it, holding it close to her chest. She stared at the trees across the river along the Kentucky bank until a bright red motorboat caught her eye. A golden retriever stood on the bow and bit at the wind in its face. Annie wished she could have a dog. She sighed as she watched the boat round the bend. It reminded her of the one Uncle Brad, Mother's younger brother, bought when they lived with Grandma Jo, before he moved north.

As Annie closed her eyes, she could see her family gathered on Grandma Jo's wide front porch, gawking at Brad standing proudly by his new toy. Grandma Jo rocked in her chair, fanning her face with delight. Annie leaped over the fence railing to touch the boat's smooth, shiny surface. Mother wiggled her cigarette at Brad, informing him he didn't have the money to pay for such a luxury item. Brad pretended he was having a coughing fit brought on by his sister's smoking. Mother shook her head in disgust and took a seat next to Grandma Jo. Brad interlocked his fingers so Annie could use them as a step to climb into the hull.

Brad owned the shiny red "luxury," as it came to be known, only long enough for him to take the family boating on the river a few times. Grandma Jo sat next to Brad as he drove, yelling at him to go faster. Faster! Mother continued her protest as she sat in the back wearing her brand new swimsuit, rubbing suntan lotion on her arms and legs. Annie remembered how it felt to sit in the front of the boat, and she wished she were sitting in the red one passing by. If she were a passenger, she'd raise her face to the sun and feel the wind blow through her hair. Instead, she sat on the steps and realized she'd be late for work if she didn't get moving.

There wasn't time for her to walk the long route home. The long route took her past the police department that tricked costumed children with apples during Halloween instead of treating them with candy, the library with one entire bookcase devoted to poetry, and the stone church that held a social every summer with a ring toss game where the prize was a two-liter bottle of pop. If she extended that route home by one block, she passed the piano teacher's house where she'd taken five lessons when she was seven paid for by Grandma Jo. (Never mind they didn't have a piano for her to practice on between the few lessons.)

Annie figured all the important places in her life could be walked to within 50 minutes-from her apartment to the dock, to the high school, to the grocery store where she worked, and back to the apartment. The plastics plant where Mother worked was not included in the tour. Annie considered the plant as part of Mother's life, not hers, even though Mother often commented how Annie benefited from the plant's dental, health, and vision insurance policies. The dentist's office was within walking distance, but it extended the "Annie's Life" walking tour 10 minutes. The eye doctor's office and general doctor's office, located on the outskirts of town, weren't part of the tour. Annie had perfect vision and didn't see the need for her to get her eyes checked so often, and she felt just plain silly stripping down to her underwear for her yearly physicals. It was because Mother was so thrilled to have insurance that she demanded Annie maintain regular appointments.

As Annie rounded the street corner with the house that appeared abandoned, the only other residence on the street as neglected as her apartment complex, she heard her mother yelling on the telephone. *The window has to be open*, she thought.

"DON'T YOU THREATEN TO HANG UP ON ME! WE ARE NOT THROUGH DISCUSSING THIS! AND WE NEED TO HURRY AND GET THIS SETTLED BEFORE I LEAVE FOR WORK!"

The entrance to Annie's apartment was on the outside of the apartment complex. Annie found the door unlocked and pushed it open wide enough for her to slide into the living room. Mother's ID badge and work bag were sprawled on the floor. Several letters (*today's mail,* Annie guessed) were spread across the coffee table. She flipped through the envelopes. *Nothing from colleges.* Granted, she hadn't requested any information from colleges, but Kelly had told her colleges began contacting students they wanted in the summer before their junior year. *I'm too average for colleges to take notice,* Annie concluded as she tossed the envelopes back onto the coffee table.

"Prick!" Mother yelled as she slammed down the receiver, her brown hair fixed for work. "Bastard hung up on me!"

"Who?" Annie asked, not sure if she wanted to know but certain she didn't want to get involved. Yet she would if need be. She and Mother were a team.

"*Your* Uncle Brad," Mother replied, dialing his number.

"What's going on?" Annie asked, opening the refrigerator to grab a bottle of water and two apples to take to work for her lunch.

"He thinks he has no part in…DON'T YOU HANG UP ON ME!" she yelled again. "He can't come here! We have no room!" Mother paused, listening. "I *know* it's only supposed to be until something opens up, but he's sick. We can't care for him like he needs!"

Annie stood at the door trying to catch Mother's eye to say good-bye. Annie waved her journal in the air to grab her mom's attention. Mother looked at the door and rolled her eyes to communicate her frustration with trying to reason with Brad. She winked at Annie and gave a brief smile before returning her attention to her telephone conversation. Annie knew Mother had lost the argument with Brad. And Mother knew it, too. *No one ever wins an argument with Brad,* Annie thought. *Mom knew it was a lost cause from the very beginning. Yet she still fought the fight. I wonder who's sick and what's going on.*

She pulled the door closed and locked it despite knowing Mother would be leaving shortly for her own shift. Annie always locked the door, even when Mother was still inside. It was a habit, and she struggled with the lock while needing to hurry, having wasted precious time waiting to catch Mother's attention. The market was an eight-minute walk, and Annie was also in the habit of waiting to leave her home precisely eight minutes before her shift began. At a brisk pace, she walked four blocks to the north, across the bridge over the old train tracks, around the corner, and across the parking lot to the store's front entrance.

It wasn't the best grocery in town. The nicer one was past the cornfield on the east side of town and was twice the size with big windows, wide aisles, and cheaper prices. The store where Annie worked had windows covered with advertisements and narrow aisles framed with tall displays of food nearly blocking the ceiling lights. But their produce selection, smaller in quantity than the eastside store, was better in quality, as it was stocked with locally grown goods. The farmers and town locals who took pride in their home-grown produce were loyal shoppers, keeping the small grocery in business.

As Annie walked in the front door, she found a young man waiting by her cash register with his arms crossed in front of his chest. *He's trying to look intimidating,* Annie thought, rolling her eyes. *He might, if he didn't look so awkward wearing fancy dress pants and a stiff white shirt with tie.* It was Cody Woods, whom Annie believed to be the worst-no, moodiest-manager in the world. *Thank goodness he graduated high school and will hopefully move away. I've had about as much of him as I can take.*

However, to his credit, Cody kept the shelves stocked and work shifts covered, but not without a snide or demeaning remark. Annie assumed his persistent bad mood was due to smoking too much pot. She didn't know for sure if he smoked it, she just assumed he did because in school he'd worn his hair dyed black and spiked, his eyes lined with mascara, and his fingernails painted with black nail polish. He and his group of goth friends were so well known that even Annie, who hardly knew anybody, would have known of Cody even if he hadn't been her manager.

"You're late," he sneered.

"No, I'm not. I'm right on time," she replied, squeezing into the cashier's booth and storing her journal and lunch on the shelf under the register. She flipped the light switch to indicate her lane was now open. "Where's Angela?" she asked.

"She left at the end of her shift, which was two minutes ago," he answered, picking his clipboard up off the price scanner.

"Well," Annie sighed, "my watch says I'm right on time." She slipped her uniform, an evergreen-colored smock, around her neck and tied it around her waist after pulling her ponytail free.

Cody held the clipboard in his hands resembling a small boy praying in church. He tilted his head and in a sappy sweet voice said, "In the future, can little Annie go by the work clock and not her wrist watch?" Dropping the tone, he continued, "I can't control everyone's personal watches."

"You can't? But you're my hero. I thought you could do *anything*," she mocked.

Cody gave her a sharp look, shook his head, and left. Annie glared at his back as he walked away.

He's such a prick, she thought. *What's the point of getting on my case for being two minutes late? It's not as though shoppers are waiting on me. I'm a good worker. I've only called in three times in the two years I've worked here.* She tried to look around the store for customers, but her vision was obstructed by the high food displays. *There aren't even any shoppers here.*

Annie opened her journal and set it on the scanner. She needed to revise a poem she wrote last month. She thought she'd finished it, but when she came across it later, the images didn't feel right. The poem was supposed to be about a magic park bench at a playground that eliminated loneliness from the lives of those who sat on it by connecting them to the people who had rested there in the past. But when she re-read her work, she envisioned a lonely bench holding no such magic. Annie studied the words, trying to understand why they didn't work together.

Entranced in her poem, she didn't notice someone had approached her register until she heard the thud of an orange juice carton hitting the conveyor belt. "Paper or plastic?" Annie asked as she set her journal and pencil to the side.

"Good afternoon, Annie. Enjoying your summer vacation?"

Annie didn't need to look up at the face to identify the voice. "Hi, Ms. Erwin," Annie said, smiling at her sophomore English teacher. "Paper or plastic?"

"Let's go with paper. I have enough plastic bags at home." She paused. "And your summer?"

"It's fine," Annie said, shrugging her shoulders.

"Are you working many hours?" Ms. Erwin asked. She took a small can of tomato paste from the cart and placed it on the conveyor belt.

"Yeah. I'm full-time when I'm out of school," Annie replied, entering the code for bananas.

"Saving your money?"

Annie blushed. Ms. Erwin was speaking to her like a mother, which she liked, despite not knowing if she should. Her own mom was perfectly capable of mothering. There just wasn't much time for it because, as a team, they were busy working together to make enough money to meet their obligations.

"Yes," Annie answered, before thinking. The truth was Annie wasn't saving her money. *Crap! Now I've lied without meaning to.* She didn't think the truth was the answer Ms. Erwin wanted to hear, and Annie had wanted to please her.

"Saving for college? It's never too early."

"Not exactly," Annie said. *How do I make things right without looking bad?* She considered for a moment. *I guess I'll just set the record straight.* "Most of my money goes to pay bills."

Ms. Erwin inspected Annie. "I thought your mom got her job back at the plastic company."

"She did. She's been back for a while," Annie answered, avoiding eye contact. "But my stepdad did her kind of wrong, and she has a lot of bills to pay off. I just help out a bit." Annie was proud of the household money she contributed. But she downplayed it because she didn't like the way Ms. Erwin looked at her.

Ms. Erwin nodded, having sensed Annie's defensiveness, and finished unloading her cart. Annie reached for the next item and discovered it was a box of tampons. She hated ringing up personal items for people she knew, such as condoms for her classmates, hemorrhoid cream for her principal, or gas relief for the bloated dentist. To deal with the embarrassment of being invited into the most personal areas of people's lives, Annie learned to act like the offending item was a mere can of corn.

"Is that a new poem you're working on?" Ms. Erwin asked, motioning to Annie's open journal.

If anyone else had asked, Annie would have denied it was a poem and changed the subject. She would have thought, *This small town is so nosey. I don't want everyone knowing about the personal poems I write!* Annie had taken great care to select an emotionless poem for the library's poetry contest, focusing on detailed images. The fact she won indicated, to her, the lack of poetry writers in the town.

But Ms. Erwin was different, almost not fitting into the town. She had been married to the high school's German teacher, who emigrated from Austria and made sure all his students knew the difference between Austria and Germany. He was the only Austrian living in the county, and old men sitting outside the auto parts store drinking their morning coffee touted him when discussing how diverse the area had become. Mr. Erwin's classroom was down the hall from his wife's, and they spent time between classes together, talking and laughing with the students walking by.

Annie was a student in Ms. Erwin's class when Mr. Erwin had a heart attack in his sleep and passed away. Annie stayed up all night writing a poem that would capture the husband and wife team talking and laughing with students. The finished product wasn't her best work; unwilling to wait, she had forced too many of the words. But it was important to Annie Ms. Erwin receive her poem before the funeral. Annie mailed the poem, without a note, to Ms. Erwin's home address, which she found in the phonebook. After Ms. Erwin returned to school, she attached a note to one of Annie's graded assignments thanking her for the beautiful poem. And yes, she had used the word *beautiful*, to Annie's delight.

"Um, yes, it's a poem," Annie said, placing a box of green tea near the top of the bag.

"Can I read it?"

Annie blushed at Ms. Erwin's interest. "When I finish it, I guess. It's not done yet."

"Please remember me when it's finished."

"Yes." There were only a few groceries left to scan and bag. The conversation would soon end.

"Are you signed up for my Honors English class in the fall?"

Annie shook her head.

"Why not?" Ms. Erwin asked, frowning more than when she had asked about Mother's job at the plant.

Annie glanced at the groceries. "I thought that class was for people planning on going to college." *I should tell her no colleges are contacting me so she'll understand.*

"The class is for *exceptional writers*," Ms. Erwin emphasized. "I think you should enroll. I also think you should consider college."

Annie totaled the bill, hoping the topic would change. Other than trying to start saving a little money to buy a car next year, she didn't like thinking about the future. As far as she could see, she didn't have any options after high school other than staying in town with her mom and entering her poems in local or regional contests. But that was okay. She couldn't think of anything else she'd rather be doing, except maybe driving her own car into the city to people watch.

Cody approached from his office located at the back of the store. Annie wished she had a fly swatter to bat him away. She didn't want him pestering Ms. Erwin. *It's one thing for him to bother me, but it's another thing for him to bother her. She doesn't need him wasting her time.*

Ms. Erwin interrupted Annie's thoughts by saying, "Why, hello, Cody! It's nice to see you. Congratulations on your graduation!" She handed money to Annie.

"Thanks," Cody replied. "Would you like help carrying your groceries to your car?"

"That would be lovely."

Annie handed Ms. Erwin her change, staring in disbelief at Cody. *Should I feel honored to witness his first pleasant moment ever*, she wondered, a thought that caused her to laugh. She covered her mouth and pretended she was coughing. Cody took the sacks in his arms and waited. He ignored Annie's laugh.

"Cody took my honors class both years, didn't you?" Ms. Erwin asked, looking at Cody. He gave a slight nod.

Ms. Erwin turned back to Annie. "Promise me you'll sign up for my class. Consider college and send me a copy of your poem when you finish. You have real talent for writing poems."

Annie smiled. "Thank you," she said before moving away to straighten her work station. Annie wished Cody hadn't heard the end of her private conversation with Ms. Erwin. *He may be nice to her, but he isn't nice to me! I hope he doesn't say something mean about my poetry. Not that I care what he thinks. I just don't want this being something else he can give me a hard time about.* As Annie wiped the condensation from the orange juice container off the conveyor belt, she had the impression Cody was still staring at her. By the time she sneaked a look, however, he had followed Ms. Erwin outside.

Chapter Three

Light from the setting sun illuminated Annie's walk home from work. She always walked home on the sidewalk on the left side of the street. The sidewalk on the other side of the street was broken in places by large tree roots, making it easy for the hurried to trip and fall. Annie tried to be more careful during the hours when the town doctor's office was closed. The nearest hospital was in the city, an hour drive away. And even though a part of Mother would be proud to flash one of the insurance cards she'd worked so hard for at the admitting receptionist, a hospital bill was one more bill they didn't need.

Annie looked down the street and saw her mom sitting outside their apartment on the concrete retaining wall, leaning her head back and blowing cigarette smoke into the air. *I wonder what's made her start smoking again. How long did she last…five weeks this time?* Annie hated when her mom smoked-a habit she'd been unsuccessful in trying to break.

"I wish I'd never started. If I could go back in time," Mother lamented.

"At least you keep trying," Annie encouraged every time.

What's she doing home, Annie now began to wonder. *She should still be at work.* Mother worked the second shift, from three to eleven, and often stayed over to see what extra hours she could pick up. Most mornings, Mother staggered through the front door after working her extra hours, dropped her ID card and duffle bag on the floor, kicked off her shoes, and collapsed into one of the kitchen chairs. Annie, an early riser by nature, stood ready with a cup of decaffeinated coffee to set in front of her.

Money hadn't always been such a need. They'd hit tough times after Annie's dad moved away and Mother fell into a depression after receiving the divorce papers. She'd held out hope he'd return and things would go back to normal. With that hope lost, Grandma Jo moved them from the city to her house, where Mother's depression seemed to worsen. After Grandma Jo threw a bucket of water on Mother while she was in bed, Mother decided she wasn't going to let some "lousy man" get her down. She went job hunting and ended up winning a prize even greater than a ring-toss two-liter bottle of pop: a job at the plastic company working on the line.

"Yes!" Mother exclaimed into the telephone. "I'll take the position! Thank you, oh, thank you!" Forgetting to hang up the phone receiver, she grabbed six-year-old Annie, lifted her into the air, and swung her around the room. She even tried lifting Grandma Jo, who laughed and said, "Child, you're gonna hurt your back and miss your first day of work." It must have been a convincing argument because Mother stopped trying and gave her a bear hug. Annie joined them. All three of them had their arms wrapped around each other, but Annie and Grandma Jo knew they were both just hugging Mother as she cried.

Then Larry, a short, stocky traveling salesman with a strong jaw, came knocking at Mother's door. After a few months of dating, he asked Mother to marry him, and she agreed, believing he was her king. Annie even looked like a princess in her bridesmaid dress at their wedding. Larry filled their castle, his apartment in the city, with treasures of pearl earrings and necklaces, expensive perfume, fancy art paintings, and a big-screen television set. He adorned the driveway with a new truck equipped with a back seat. Mother was happy to quit her job to take care of her king. However, after years of Larry's extended business trips, Mother learned her castle was built on sand and all her treasures were bought on credit in her name. Then Mother learned the "business" that kept Larry out of town was a woman named Sally who lived in Illinois.

The city lawyer Mother hired for the second divorce sent her further into debt. After all the fighting and yelling during the break-up, Annie was delighted to move with her mom back into Grandma Jo's house in the peaceful country. Soon after the divorce finalized, Grandma Jo died in her sleep from complications of diabetes and Mother entered into an even deeper depression. She didn't leave her bed. She didn't even chain smoke. Brad, who came home for the funeral, had to sell the house to pay Grandma Jo's debts. He even stayed in town a few extra weeks while Mother gathered herself and found their apartment. Luckily, Annie had just turned 14 and was able to get a job at the grocery store to pay the measly rent.

The final push to Mother's rolling out of bed and reaching for her lighter was Annie bringing papers home from school stating the school required students to have health insurance. It was the only time Annie felt happy seeing her mom smoke a cigarette. The fire she'd lit in Mother caused Mother to become determined to regain her job at the plant. After two private meetings with the human resources lady, Mother resumed her coveted position on the line. This time, she vowed to never give it up. *There aren't many people who could do what she's done, faced with the hardships and heartache she's suffered,* Annie swore.

"What're you doing home so early?" Annie asked as she crossed the street and sat on the retaining wall next to Mother. Annie wiped the sweat from her brow. *Humid,* she thought. *I don't usually sweat walking home.* Mother exhaled a breath of smoke.

"I didn't go in today. I'm going to work the first shift tomorrow." She took a drag on her cigarette. "Your uncle's a bastard," she proclaimed, holding in her breath. "He's caused me to start smoking again."

"What's going on?" Annie asked because it was unusual for Mother to talk to Brad on the telephone other than on Thanksgiving and Christmas. When Grandma Jo was alive, Mother and Brad's relationship was closer, despite Mother's constant unsolicited advice about his job, the girls he dated, and even the food he ate. Brad would catch Annie's eye during Mother's lectures and make silly faces. More than once, Annie had to run from the room to avoid laughing out loud. Even after moving to the northern part of the state, Brad visited them at Grandma Jo's house several times a year. Annie had assumed in error Brad would continue to visit after Grandma Jo passed.

"Gordon's group home is closing," Mother answered, releasing a stream of smoke as she spoke. She flicked the ashes off the end of her cigarette. It took Annie a moment to remember Gordon was Mother's older brother. He was disabled, with mental retardation and autism, and had lived in a home most of his life. "Since Brad lives closest to him, he's going to pick him up tomorrow and bring him here."

"Here?" Annie was dubious, twisting to look around at their small two-bedroom apartment.

"I know! I told Brad we didn't have the room. He wouldn't budge about me being the one to take him. He said since I'm a woman, I'll know better what to do. I told him since he's a man, he can relate better to Gordon. He said I'm closer to Gordon because I'm older and spent more time with him before he went into the home…and on and on. Bottom line, I can't turn Gordon away. He's family."

"Isn't he dangerous?" Annie countered in a voice that was a bit too loud, indicating her worry. Gordon might be family, but he was also a stranger. Annie hadn't seen him since she was a young girl, when the whole family piled into the car and drove for hours to Gordon's group home. It was the only visit she remembered. Gordon had become upset, and the manager said the visit caused more harm than good and asked they not visit anymore. But Grandma Jo didn't want Gordon thinking his family had abandoned him, so she began calling him on the phone, even though Gordon couldn't talk.

"He can at least listen to me telling him I love him," Grandma Jo pleaded into the phone to one of the group home staff.

"He's deaf. You have to learn to accept that. The phone calls do no good."

"Damn you! He can too hear!" Grandma Jo asserted. But, in time, the phone calls stopped, too.

Annie knew Gordon as the face in the framed photograph sitting on the kitchen shelf and as the name on the box of shirts she and Mother mailed to his group home every Christmas. But foremost in Annie's mind, as she sat with Mother on the retaining wall in the humid night air, she knew Gordon as the teenager Grandma Jo had sent to live in a group home because she couldn't control him. When he became angry, he ran wild, oblivious to his own strength as he knocked things over in the house. Yes, Annie was worried, and she knew she sounded panicked.

"Now, honey, calm down," Mother soothed, patting Annie on the knee. "Do you think I'd let him come into our home if he were dangerous? He's too sick now to be much of a handful. But we have to do this. Especially after everything he's been through." She put out her cigarette on the retaining wall, tossed it out onto the road, and lit another one. The sun had now set.

"What's he been through?" Annie asked, trying to sound calmer.

"After I got off the phone with Brad, I called someone at the state disability office. The group home is closing to avoid an investigation into allegations of abuse by staff." She took a drag on her cigarette. "This is probably the first time I can say

I'm glad Grandma Jo has passed. She always felt guilty about putting him there. You know, the doctors told her to put him in a home right after he was born. But she didn't. She kept her baby home as long as she could." Mother exhaled. "And there I was, always telling her she did the best thing for him by giving him up. And then the staff told us he was doing better *not* seeing us than when he did see us. How were we to know? They're the experts. We just wanted to do what was best. And now I find out he may have been abused." She shook her head.

"What do you mean by he's sick?" Annie asked, going back to the comment made earlier and ignoring what Mother said about the abuse, still not convinced she didn't need to worry.

"He's in the final stage of leukemia."

That's right, Annie remembered. *I knew that.*

Mother continued, "Actually, he's been in the final stage for two years. But he never was one to listen to anyone. So even though the doctors tell him he's dying, he keeps right on living."

Annie searched her mind for the bit of information she had about Gordon. She knew he was autistic. She remembered during the one family visit, he didn't act like he knew who they were or that they were even there to see him. He sat at his desk, in his bedroom, and colored a bunch of circles drawn on a white piece of paper. The rest of the family sat in a row on the edge of his bed. Grandma Jo patted his head and rubbed his back while she talked to him. *I think she might have been on the verge of crying.* But it made no difference to Gordon, who colored as though he were alone in the room. Brad had become angry and stole Gordon's crayons off the desk.

"Pay attention to your mother!" he yelled into Gordon's ear.

The reaction Brad procured from taking the crayons proved Gordon knew he had visitors. Gordon reached for the crayons, but Brad, being more than a foot taller, held them out of reach. Mother yelled, "Stop it, Brad! He doesn't understand! Give him back his crayons!" Grandma Jo wiped the tears that spilled down her cheeks. Realizing he couldn't reach the crayons held above his head, Gordon picked up his hairbrush and electric razor from the top of his dresser and threw them across the room into the wall. Frightened, Annie hid behind the closet door. One staff member removed Gordon from the room and another held Grandma Jo's hand in her own and suggested they not visit for a while.

Annie also knew Gordon didn't talk. He never learned how. He made odd noises that sounded like angry animals… ferocious growls and daring, high-pitched squeaks and squawks. Doctors attributed Gordon's inability to talk and odd noises to his being deaf. Yet Grandma Jo, Mother, and Brad maintained that anyone who spent any time with Gordon knew he was stubborn, not deaf. "When that doctor tells me Gordon's deaf, and I know he's not, it makes it hard to believe anything else he has to say!" Grandma Jo exclaimed in disgust.

Mother continued, "Anyway, the guy from the state said it should only be a few days until they find a new group home. But I told him it shouldn't be just any home. It should be someplace close to a hospital…since he's sick and all."

Annie nodded. *It'll be okay. He'll only be here for a few days.* She gave a sigh of relief and tried to envision how a sick Gordon might look, pale and weak. *Mother is clever to think about the hospital.* Now knowing Gordon's stay would be limited to a few days, Annie experienced a twinge of guilt. *He is my uncle, after all. Just like Brad. I wouldn't have been scared to have Brad stay with us for a few days. But then Brad didn't have to be sent to a home to be controlled. But Gordon is sick, so it's different. He'll probably sleep all the time, like I do when I'm sick. Things will be fine. It's only for a few days.*

The ashes on the end of Mother's cigarette were longer than the filter. She put the cigarette out on the retaining wall and tossed it into the street, where it landed close to the one she'd tossed earlier. She reached into her carton for another one, but the carton was empty. Mother swore. "Anyway… after I hung up with the man from the state, I gave the whole thing some thought. I don't like the idea of him being moved to a group home so far from us, like he is now. I want him to be close. Grandma Jo would want that, too. I called the guy from the state back and told him to try to find a group home down here by us. He said it might take a little longer to get him into a home, but I said that was fine. I called Brad back to see what he thought. He thinks Gordon should stay with us until we find a closer home."

"But, Mom!" Annie exclaimed, her anxiety returning. "It's hard to cover our expenses now! We can't afford a third person!" She didn't let guilt stop her from stating her concerns. *I would have had the same worry if Brad stayed with us,* she justified.

"We can cover for a little while."

"Where will he sleep?" Annie demanded.

Mother crumpled the cigarette carton in her hand. Annie could tell she wanted another one. Then Mother pointed at Kelly's house. "What's that?"

A small light flickered on and off in the darkened upstairs window facing the street. Kelly had told Annie her bedroom window overlooked the street.

"I think Kelly's trying to get our attention," Annie guessed.

"You know one of those religious freaks?" Mother asked, turning to look at Annie.

How can you not know that we talk every now and then? But she said, "Only the daughter. She's not so bad. She just says what she's heard." Annie gave a little wave in the direction of the window. The flickering light stopped.

"What does she want?" Mother asked.

"To be noticed," Annie responded. But she wasn't through talking about Gordon. "So where's he going to sleep?"

"Right," Mother said, as though she had forgotten. "Here's what I've planned. Tomorrow, late morning, Linda is going to bring by a mattress and bed frame. I think we should move your mattress into my room so he can have his own room. Since he's sick, he should have his own space. Brad will bring him down tomorrow night. You don't work tomorrow, right?"

"Right," Annie replied through clenched teeth, her sympathy gone. She did not appreciate having to give up her bedroom. *He's only a guest*, she rationalized. *He can sleep on the couch. That's where Brad would stay. I pay part of the rent. I should have the bedroom. He's retarded! He can't even talk! He won't notice not having his own room, anyhow.*

Mother ignored the forcefulness of Annie's response. "Well, on Monday and Tuesday, Linda will stay with him while we work. I let her borrow my truck twice. Remember? She borrowed it once to move her into her house and then to move her son to Kentucky. She's going to help with Gordon to return the favor. You have Wednesday off work, right?

"Right," Annie fumed. "Isn't Linda a little irresponsible? She's living with a drunk and can't keep a job herself!"

"But she'll help us for free on this short of notice." Without skipping a beat, Mother continued, "And Thursday and Friday I'm off work. So, hopefully, the state will have something lined up by then. They'll have almost a week."

"Sounds like a plan," Annie said. Keeping her teeth clenched was starting to hurt her jaw. *A plan that benefits you, not me*, she thought.

"Coming in?" Mother asked. She stood and yawned, stretching her arms over her head. "First shift is going to be here before I know it." A streak of lightning crossed the sky. "Well, I'm not surprised. It's humid enough for the rain," Mother said.

It was no use arguing. Annie knew Mother's mind was made up. *So much for us being a team.* Annie stood and followed Mother to their door. Before Annie stepped inside, she looked at Kelly's darkened window. Feeling resentful and assuming Kelly's private bedroom was twice the size of the one Annie was about to lose, she mimicked, *Did you thank God for your own room tonight?* A loud clap of thunder sounded as Annie closed and locked the door.

Chapter Four

Beads of rain hit Annie's bedroom window throughout the night, but Annie couldn't hear them over the thoughts of injustice pounding against her skull. *Why did Mom go through the trouble of finding Gordon a bed frame when she lets me sleep on a mattress on the floor?* She tossed and turned, tangling herself in the thin summer sheet. *He can hear. Mom said so. He takes advantage of people by ignoring them. He does what he wants, which is coloring, of all things. He could live on his own. People overcome adversity all the time. But he won't even try to better himself, so I have to suffer.*

Trapped in bed, she lay victim to her fear. *What if we can't support all three of us and Mom goes back into her depression? I can't care for both of them. I won't. Brad isn't going to help. I'd have to drop out of school. Well, I'll be 16, and that's when I can drop out. Maybe I can support them both if I work full-time year-round.*

By morning, the storm had passed. Though the sun had risen, the rain had cooled the air and the wet earth looked cold. Annie freed herself from her sheet and slipped on a hooded sweatshirt and a pair of jeans with one of the knees ripped out. Standing in the bathroom, she could hear Mother snoring. *Great. I'll have to sleep with that now*, she thought. She brushed her teeth and pulled her long hair into a ponytail. She grabbed her journal and closed the front door behind her without making a noise. She needed the dock. She needed to escape, time to make sense of things.

Large puddles had formed in the streets and on the sidewalks. If it had been any other morning, Annie would have jumped into one of the puddles so she could feel her wet cotton socks stick to her feet and hear her sneakers make squishing sounds with each step. But not that day. She didn't want out-of-the-ordinary experiences. She wanted her dull, routine life, and she wanted reassurance her dull, routine life wouldn't change.

Outside the stone church, children gathered before the early service to inspect whether any playground equipment was dry enough to play on without dirtying their Sunday clothes. The adult parishioners gathered at the front sidewalk to talk about how much rain they'd received and how it would affect this year's crops. Annie marveled at how the majority of men in town looked the same. There was some variety in the hair styles, clothing, and shoes of the town women and children. But the men varied only in hairstyle as the young men fashioned buzz cuts and the elders wore short styles where the hair lay flat on their heads. The young and old alike wore industrial-looking jackets and coats with dark blue "dress-up" jeans and work boots. The only men in town who didn't mirror the men outside the church were the few black men…and Cody Woods and his goth friends.

Annie crossed the street so she wouldn't be mistaken for someone attending the service. Besides, she didn't feel she fit into their crowd, even though she may have looked like them. *Cody Woods kept his individuality in school. Spiked black hair and wrists and arms covered with leather bracelets and tattoos.*

Even when he tries to fit in by wearing white button-up shirts and ties for work, he sticks out. Surely he has the sense to know he looks different. He must really want to dress in black 'cause I'm sure he's not able to buy his clothes new from any of the little stores here. Perhaps that's why he's chronically moody. He doesn't know how to fit in, Annie diagnosed. Then she thought about Gordon. *Does he know he's different? Does he know it's not normal to live in a group home?*

Annie reached the dock. Like the children at the church playground, Annie was unable to find a dry surface. She contemplated sitting on top of her journal on the steps, but she didn't want to get it wet. She had brought it only out of habit. She had no desire to create a new poem or edit an old one. She needed to clear her mind and heart of the weighty thoughts and emotions she still carried with her from last night. She walked down the steps, in the direction of the water, to lean against the guardrail separating the parking lot from the rocky embankment that met the river's edge. The wind off the river was strong. The cold bit at Annie's cheeks and nose. She was glad it did. It took her mind off the heaviness of her heart.

"You have to pray to God for what you want." Kelly's words echoed in Annie's mind. She closed her eyes. *Fine,* Annie conceded, feeling desperate. *Dear God, what I want is for Gordon to NOT stay with us. I'm afraid he'll destroy what little Mom and I have. And I feel bad for not wanting him to come. Grandma Jo would be disappointed in me. She took me in when Mom and I had nowhere to go. But this is different. Mom and I aren't dangerous. He is, or at least, he might be. And even though he's sick, he's been sick for years. So that doesn't mean anything.* She sighed. *But he's coming. I know. So please look after me and Mom. Keep us safe. Help Mom to be strong. Sorry this doesn't sound like a preacher's prayer.*

Annie opened her eyes. She stared at the choppy water below. A buoy up the river bobbed in the waves, low in the water but not submerged. *That's what I need to do. I need to be a buoy for Mom. I shouldn't make things worse for her.*

Like being upset about giving up my room. I don't need to worry her. I need to make sure things go well with Gordon. That would make Grandma Jo proud of me, too.

Finding a purpose, relief flooded over Annie, shocking her as though she were standing in the cold river instead of looking down upon it. She smiled. *This praying thing helps,* she admitted. *Oh, one more thing, God. I'm sorry I called Cody a prick yesterday…and all the other times, too. I know I'm supposed to love others like you love me, or something like that,* she confessed for safe measure. She wished Kelly had elaborated on whether prayer had to include confession in order for God to hear it.

With a warmer heart, Annie started home. Mother would already be at work by the time Annie returned. Annie began composing a list of things she needed to do to get the apartment ready for Gordon. She decided to surprise Mother by giving the apartment a thorough cleaning. *What better way to show her my support?* she reasoned. Not only would Annie straighten up the clutter in the living room, kitchen, and her bedroom, but she would clean from ceiling to floor, even dusting the pictures hanging on the walls and wiping the baseboards that bordered the apartment.

As she passed back by the stone church, the music flowing out the open door caught her attention. The congregation was singing with the choir. Annie approached the side door, careful to stay hidden from view of those inside. Wrapping her arms around her journal, she leaned her forehead against the rough, stone doorframe to listen. She thought the music was beautiful and stayed long enough to hear the song's end. Then she hurried home to start completing the tasks on her list. The thought of entering the church for the remainder of the service never crossed her mind.

Chapter Five

A series of loud knocks on the door announced the arrival of Gordon's bed frame and mattress. Annie was in the bathroom scrubbing the soap buildup off the tub. She quickened her pace so she could finish before answering the door, but she abandoned her efforts at the second series of loud knocks. *Good grief. Give me a minute, will you?* She took off her yellow rubber gloves and set them on the edge of the tub. She wiped the sweat from her brow with her forearm as she searched in her pocket for the key. She opened the door to find Linda standing on her tiptoes, leaning over the side of the porch rail, straining to look in the window.

"I didn't think you were home," Linda said, motioning to Gary to start unloading the furniture.

"Sorry. I was in the back, cleaning," Annie replied.

"No bother. Where do you want my bed to go?" Linda asked, trying to squeeze her round body and equally round grey, frizzy hair through the small gap between Annie and the door.

Annie took a step back to make way. She didn't doubt Linda would run her over, if necessary, to enter the apartment.

"In my room," Annie said. "This way." She led Linda to her bedroom. Linda surveyed the mattress on the floor. Gary appeared behind them with the headboard. A cigarette hung out of his mouth.

"In there." Linda pointed. "Annie, I swore your mama said she needed a bed and a mattress."

"She does," Annie replied. She walked into her room and pulled the loose sheet off the mattress. Grasping the middle of the mattress, she stood it on its side. "This is mine. I'm going to move it into Mom's room."

"Ya don't have a frame?" Linda asked. Gary edged past Linda and leaned the headboard against the wall. Annie shook her head, trying to ignore the sore spot Linda's question touched. She wanted Gary and Linda to leave the room so she could pull the mattress across the hall into Mother's room. Gary left to retrieve another piece of the frame. As he walked past, Annie tried to breathe in to see if he smelled of alcohol. He didn't. *Good.*

She turned her attention back to Linda, who hadn't taken the hint Annie was waiting for her to leave. Linda stopped at the dresser to pick up Annie's little jewelry box to study it. As Annie looked at the back of Linda's head, she heard Linda smacking the gum she was chewing. Finally, Linda wandered into the hall, allowing Annie space to pull her thin mattress into Mother's room. *I'll move Mom's stuff around to make a place for my stuff later,* she reasoned, kicking some of the clothes on the floor out of her way.

She entered the living room and found Linda sitting on the couch, her feet propped up on the coffee table. It was clear she wasn't going to help with the bed. "Do ya have anything to drink?" she asked, blowing a bubble so big it popped on her face. She used her fingers to pick the pieces of gum off her chin and nose before putting them back in her mouth.

"We have regular pop that might be flat, and we have water. I'm going to the store after I clean." Gary walked by with the two sideboards. Annie asked him, "Do you want me to help?"

"With the mattress." He disappeared into her room.

"Ya don't have diet pop?" Linda asked.

"No."

"I just don't have a liking for flat Coke. Never developed the taste. Water will do. I started a new allergy medicine, and it dries my mouth out something horrible!"

Annie reached into the refrigerator for the gallon of water she used to fill her water bottles for work. One of the perks of working for the grocery store was she could refill her gallon jug in the fancy water purifier machine for only 20 cents instead of the 39 cents other customers paid. Annie poured Linda a small glass of water because she wanted them to leave after assembling the bed frame.

"Thanks, hon! Where do I leave the tip?" Linda joked. She took the glass and finished the water, to Annie's delight, in one long drink.

Annie propped the door open with a loose brick from the front porch and followed Gary outside. He hopped into the truck bed and pushed the mattress over to Annie. It was a thick mattress and hard for Annie to hold, but not heavy enough for Gary to need help. *Perhaps he wants my help to maneuver it through the cramped living room and narrow hall to the bedroom. Maybe he's afraid he'll knock over a lamp or a picture off the wall.* Annie appreciated his respect for their things, even though nothing they owned was fancy or new. His consideration surprised her. Knowing him as one of the town's drunks caused her to think he only cared about alcohol.

"Do you need any tools to put the frame together?" she asked as they walked into her bedroom.

"Nope. The pieces fit together like a puzzle."

"Annie," Linda yelled, "come in here and tell me about Gordon. I'm gonna sit with him tomorrow for your mama.

She asked if I could, and I said, 'Sure.' I'm not one to abandon someone in their time of need, you know."

Annie didn't know, but she smiled politely all the same as she left the mattress in Gary's hands and retrieved Gordon's picture from the kitchen shelf.

"Oh my Lord!" Linda hooted. "Look at your mama's hair! Gary, come here and look at this old picture."

Gary stuck his head out of the bedroom. "Yup," he said to humor Linda. He didn't even look at the picture before returning to the frame. Annie followed Gary back into the bedroom. She stood between the two sideboards and lifted them, keeping them level, so Gary could fit them into the footboard.

"I can see the family resemblance," Linda hollered, still chuckling. "What's he like?"

Annie didn't want to share her one memory of hiding in the closet while Gordon colored, Grandma Jo cried, and Mother yelled at Brad, who yelled at Gordon. "I only visited when I was a kid and too young to remember. He's quiet. He doesn't talk. I guess that doesn't tell you much," she yelled into the living room.

Gary now fit the headboard onto the sideboards. Annie stepped out of the middle of the bed and walked back into the living room.

"That's okay," Linda said, leaning forward to set the picture on the coffee table. "What'll ya have for lunch tomorrow?"

Annie hadn't thought about it. "Sandwiches, I guess, unless there's something else you'd rather have."

"Sandwiches are fine but can ya be sure to have some mustard? I don't like mayo, and sandwiches can be so dry without something. Oh, you done, honey?"

Gary had emerged from the bedroom. Annie picked up an ashtray off the table and held it out to him. He put out his cigarette as Annie held the tray.

"Thanks," he nodded. "I'm ready."

Linda hoisted herself off the couch. "What time should I be here tomorrow?"

"Mom goes into work at 2:30. She'll want to introduce you to Gordon and talk to you about a few things. So come a little earlier?"

"That's fine," she said, smacking her gum and following Gary to the truck.

"Thank you!" Annie called out from the door.

Linda leaned her head out of the window as the truck rolled toward the street. "Can ya get some diet pop at the store for me?"

Annie nodded and watched the truck round the corner. She shut the door. She picked up Gordon's picture off the coffee table and returned it to the kitchen shelf. *I better add Linda's requests to the grocery list before I forget*. She rummaged through the junk drawer under the telephone for a pen or pencil. She wrote down the items on the list Mother had started earlier in the week. Before she left the list to return to cleaning the bathroom, she reviewed it, stumbling over the item "diapers."

Annie frowned. *Mom didn't say anything about being invited to a baby shower. Besides, there isn't a baby shower invitation stuck behind a magnet*, she reasoned, looking at the refrigerator. *Getting diapers doesn't make sense. The list is for the few items we might need this week for Gordon… Gordon. Oh my goodness*, Annie thought, her eyes widening as she looked at the list. *Does Gordon wear diapers? Is there such a thing as diapers for adults? There must be. People can be in comas and not able to walk to the bathroom. Why not for people never toilet trained?* Annie hoped the grocery store carried them. She never shopped in the baby aisle because there'd never been a need.

Annie put her yellow rubber gloves back on and finished scrubbing the tub before directing her attention to the living room. She picked the mail up off the floor, throwing away the coupons they wouldn't use. She snatched up a crumpled napkin by the edge of the sofa before vacuuming. She grabbed a rag and wiped the television screen and coffee table, the only items of furniture needing to be dusted. Then, she approached Mother's bedroom. She threw the clothes strewn about the floor into the closet, forming a pile so tall it almost met the bottom edges of the shirts hanging above. She pushed Mother's mattress closer to the wall and laid her own flat on the floor next to it. She retrieved her sheet and pillow from her room. She'd make her bed later.

It was time to convert her bedroom into a guest room. She retrieved a fresh set of sheets from the hall closet and sulked into her room. *It's only temporary,* she reminded herself, making up the new bed. Then she opened her closet door and stared at her clothes. *Where do I move them? There's no room in Mom's closet.* She closed the door. *He can live out of a suitcase for a week. He probably doesn't even have nice clothes that need hanging, So then he wouldn't need a dresser drawer, either.* Her "to do" list for her bedroom was shrinking. The only thing left for Annie to do was to remove the items she wanted to protect, just in case Gordon was still in the habit of throwing things. *I don't want my things destroyed.*

After loading up her arms with her belongings and not knowing where to store them, she decided to only take the few things she treasured most and returned what she held in her arms. She opened the nightstand drawer and removed the old black-and-white photograph of Grandma Jo trimming Brad's hair in the yard while Mother sat in a lawn chair holding her dog, Frisky. *Grandpa must have taken the picture.* It hadn't struck her, until now, that Gordon wasn't in the picture. *Mom and Brad are young. Gordon must still be living at home. Maybe he was inside the house coloring.* Annie continued sifting through the drawer.

She also wanted to keep the letter the hunky Hollywood star, Matthew Charles, sent her in response to a fan letter she had written him for a school project. His letter had an original signature, indicating his hands had touched it. Annie never felt so glamorous, after getting off the bus and retrieving the letter from Grandma Jo's mailbox and walking up the lane reading his words. *To think, someone from Hollywood thought enough about me to respond to my letter and address the envelope, stamp it, and put it in the mail. The whole process must have lasted at least 20 minutes!* For 20 minutes, heartthrob Matthew Charles thought about her!

With the photograph and letter in one hand, Annie pulled open the bottom dresser drawer to retrieve her two old journals. She pushed the drawer closed with her foot. She slipped the photograph and letter into the front cover of one of the journals and walked into Mother's room. Annie picked up the edge of her thin mattress and laid the journals side-by-side underneath it. She looked at her watch. She needed to hurry to the grocery store. She wanted to be back when Mother arrived home from work and remarked about how clean the apartment looked. Mother's compliments reminded Annie of when she was five years old and had just been handed a bag of pink and blue cotton candy at the little summer carnival set up for a week alongside the river.

Annie grabbed the grocery list and pen off the kitchen counter and took some money from the cookie jar. She pulled the apartment door shut and locked it with her key. As she hurried to the store, she wrote numbers next to the items on the list so she could gather them in order as she strolled up and down the aisles. She wasn't sure which number to put in front of the diapers, so she circled the item as she stepped on the black, plastic mat, triggering the store's automatic door to open. With her head down to find number one on the list, she almost walked into a crowd of people standing inside the front of the store.

Surprised, Annie saw several employees standing by Edna's register. Cody Woods was among them, holding a white sheet cake Annie assumed was from the store's bakery. "Good-bye Edna" was written on the cake in green icing. The white icing matched Edna's snow-white hair. Edna clasped her hands together under her chin and beamed at the employees standing around her clapping. *Her retirement party!* In Annie's haste to prepare their home for company on her day off, she had forgotten she promised Edna she'd make a special trip in to celebrate. Annie caught Cody's eye as she slipped the grocery list into her pocket and slid into the mix at Edna's side. Edna turned to see who had snuck beside her.

"Oh, Annie!" she exclaimed, hugging her. "You came! I'm so happy!"

Edna and Grandma Jo had been close friends since childhood, even once competing as younger women for Grandpa's affections. At Grandma Jo's funeral, Annie heard Edna tell Mother she was looking for part-time work to keep her busy during the day while her son and daughter-in-law were at work. When Annie obtained her job at the store, she put in a good word for Edna to Louise, one of the other store managers, encouraging her to hire Edna as a part-time cashier. During the time they worked together, Edna, who didn't yet have grandchildren, adopted Annie as her own.

"Of course I'm here!" Annie exclaimed, hugging Edna back.

Cody set the cake down on the conveyer. "Thank you for your service, Edna. We'll miss you," he said in a stiff manner.

It's so hard for him to be nice, Annie thought. *Oh well. At least he's trying.*

"Annie, you cut the cake," Edna pleaded, placing a plastic knife in Annie's hand. "I'd just mess it up." Annie cut several pieces and passed them out to their co-workers. After eating enough green icing to cause her teeth to become the color of a ripe lime, Annie gave Edna another hug. She grabbed a cart and started to maneuver it around the store to collect the items on her list. Once she found the last one, numbered 12, she reviewed the list to make sure she had everything.

The diapers! I almost forgot, she scolded herself while looking at the circled item. She steered the cart down the baby aisle and stopped in front of the diapers. Pictures of little kids adorned the wrappers. Annie frowned. She was sure any package advertising a child's face contained diapers too small for an adult.

"Are congratulations in order?" a coy voice asked.

Annie looked behind her to see Cody smirking.

"No," she replied, disgusted at being interrupted. She was pressed for time. "I don't even have a boyfriend," she threw over her shoulder, making sure he could hear her but not see her discolored teeth.

"You don't need a boyfriend."

Annie looked at him in disbelief. "What kind of girl do you think I am?" she snapped, offended. For a moment, she thought he looked surprised she was angry. *Or maybe he doesn't understand why my teeth are green.* She shook her head. *Jerk.* She sighed. "Is Edna still here? I need some help with something."

Edna could help her with the diapers. She knew Grandma Jo during Gordon's birth and admission to the group home. Annie wouldn't have to waste time explaining the situation. She also wouldn't have to feel embarrassed her uncle couldn't use a toilet.

"Edna left with half the cake right after you started shopping."

Darn. There goes that idea. Annie looked at her list, hoping Cody would leave. He didn't.

"It sure was nice of you to come in *for Edna* on your day off." He pushed the cart so it rolled, hitting Annie in her side.

She closed her eyes and took a deep breath to keep from losing her cool. She didn't have time for this. She needed to hurry. "Since you're working, maybe you can help me out." Her words didn't sound as smart and cold as she had intended. However, she did take pleasure in ending his fun.

"What do you need?" he asked, bored.

Shit. I'm going to have to tell him. "Diapers, or something like diapers, that fit adults." She held her hand up to stop the smirk forming on the side of his mouth. "For someone who's disabled…it's not funny."

The smirk vanished. "This way," he said, back to sounding bored. He led her to another aisle. "Here you go." He waved his hand across several brands of "protective underwear." Annie stood in front of the brands. *Which one do I pick?*

"Go with the generic ones with the indicator strip in the front so you, or someone, can easily tell when it's wet," he advised, walking out of the aisle.

Annie watched him leave, surprised. *How would he know anything about adult diapers? Well, for the price of the generic brand, Mom will be happy and an indicator strip would be helpful.* She threw a package into the cart.

Annie opened a register to check herself out. The extra two-liter of pop for Linda made the groceries too heavy to carry. She'd have to push the cart home and bring it back tomorrow at the start of her shift. She bagged and loaded the groceries. As she steered the cart out of the store and across the parking lot for home, she checked to see if Cody was following her, prepared to confront her about taking store property. *That would be something he'd do…pretend to help and then make things worse.* But he was nowhere to be seen.

Chapter Six

The praise Annie expected for the clean apartment didn't come. After closing but not locking the door, Mother collapsed onto the couch. She slipped off her tennis shoes and curled into a ball, pulling the throw blanket Annie had folded across the back of the couch down around her. "My body can't do these early shifts," she whined as she drifted off to sleep. Annie didn't take offense. She sat at the kitchen table, working in her journal on her magical park bench poem. Before long, the air was filled with the sound of Mother's deep snores. *She'll notice the clean apartment when she wakes up,* Annie thought, smiling.

When it was time to start fixing dinner, Annie tucked her pencil into her journal and washed and strained the lettuce for a mandarin orange and spinach salad. She opened a can of black beans for Mother to add to her salad. After watching the lump of beans drop out of the can and into the small serving bowl, Annie pushed the bowl across the table to Mother's place and added only shredded mozzarella cheese to her salad. She pulled two pieces of bread off the loaf and placed the butter on the table between their two plates.

Annie woke Mother, who stood and stumbled down the hall and into the bathroom to freshen up. On her way back to the kitchen, Mother stopped in the living room to pick up the ashtray off the coffee table. She sat down at the kitchen table and lit a cigarette before pouring raspberry vinaigrette onto her salad. The air filled with the clinks of their forks against their plates, the rattle of ice in their glasses as they drank, and the rustle of their napkins when they wiped their mouths.

Then Mother broke the silence. "I take it you're still upset with me?"

Annie shrugged her shoulders. *I hoped you'd notice I spent the day cleaning the apartment for Gordon,* she wanted to say. But she didn't. They continued to eat in silence. After taking a long drink, Mother set her glass down on the table with a thud and looked at Annie.

"I'm sorry about your bedroom. I could tell you were upset last night, but I thought you'd be over it by now."

Annie opened her mouth to protest, but Mother raised her hand to silence her.

"I didn't plan this, and it's only temporary."

Annie felt foolish and wanted to defend herself. She wanted to point out to Mother she was wrong, that Annie had changed her attitude. *Just look at the clean apartment for proof!* But Mother kept talking. Annie looked into her mother's eyes and maintained her gaze. *At least I can show her I'm listening.*

"I'm going to need your help, Annie. We're going to have to work together, be a team, to support Gordon."

Mother's eyes pleaded for an agreement. Annie nodded, "Yes, I agree, and I'm sorry about last night."

Mother shook her head. "No need to apologize. Let's just start fresh."

"Is there anything you want me to do before they come?" Annie asked, hoping she wouldn't have to point out her hard work cleaning the apartment.

Mother looked around the kitchen and living room. "Nothing comes to mind right now. We just need to work together as things come up."

They went back to eating in silence. *Don't get upset she didn't notice. You're a big girl. You don't need accolades.* Annie decided to change the subject.

"Are you nervous?" Annie asked. The last time Mother smoked through dinner was when she was anxious and worried Larry would fight the divorce, which he threatened to do, but never followed through.

"A bit. If Grandma Jo had a hard time caring for him, then I'm not sure how I'm going to be able to do it."

Deciding not to share she held similar fears, Annie offered, "But you're not alone. You have me!"

Mother gave a tired smile. She leaned forward to pat Annie's arm.

After they ate and between puffs on her cigarette, Mother dried the dishes Annie washed and put them away. The apartment had a dishwasher, but its water jets were too weak to knock the food particles off the dishes. Mother called the leasing office to complain, but the manager never replaced it. He didn't even send someone over to look at it. Annie had determined for the dishwasher to work, they would have to wash all the dishes by hand first. If they washed the dishes by hand first, then there was no need for the dishwasher. So they only ran the dishwasher, without dishes, every other week to keep it from smelling foul.

The tension Annie felt earlier toward her mother was gone, replaced by the anxiety from knowing Gordon would be there soon.

"Was Gary sober?" Mother asked, interrupting the silence.

"Seemed to be," Annie replied, rinsing the soap suds off a plate.

"I'm surprised Linda puts up with it."

"Well, I'm not sure how much of a walk in the park she is,"

Annie said. Mother nodded and put the small glass Annie had filled for Linda in the cupboard.

Later while Annie was sweeping the floor, she said, "Today was Edna's last day at the store. They threw her a little party."

"Did you go?" Mother asked.

"Yes," Annie replied. *Great, now she'll think I was socializing all day instead of cleaning.* So she added, "I only stayed at the party for a few minutes before I picked up our groceries."

Shortly after nine o'clock, there was a series of knocks on the door. Neither Annie nor Mother moved from the couch, as though they couldn't imagine who it could be. After the second series of knocks, Mother stood to open the door. Annie reached for the remote control and turned off the television. Mother paused before opening the door. *There's no going back now,* Annie thought.

Brad stood square in the doorway, tall and skinny as ever. His brown hair was longer than Annie remembered. *But then, it's been almost two years since I've seen him,* she justified. One of his large hands was wrapped around a garbage bag and the other hand was wrapped around Gordon's small hand. Gordon stood behind Brad. Annie couldn't see him until they stepped inside the apartment.

"Hello! Come in!" Mother exclaimed with forced enthusiasm. She closed the door behind them and wrapped her arm around Brad's side with the garbage bag, giving him a tiny squeeze. "Still no meat on these bones! You need to find yourself a woman who'll cook for you," she joked.

"Yeah, yeah, yeah…I've heard it all before," Brad replied, smiling. "I take it you're still smoking those stupid things?"

"What makes you think that?" Mother asked, leaning back to look at him. She wasn't holding a cigarette.

Brad raised his eyebrow and shook his head. Annie knew how he knew. The apartment reeked of cigarette smoke. "I was hoping you'd quit," he replied.

"I did for six weeks…until all this happened."

Brad held out the garbage bag for Annie to take. He winked at her and kissed Mother on the top of her head. Mother released Brad and tried to peer around him to see Gordon. Brad dropped Gordon's hand and stepped to the side, saying, "No need to be shy, boy. Step out here where they can see you."

Annie was surprised to discover Gordon was no taller than she. She'd assumed he shared Mother and Brad's height. *I guess I was a lot smaller when I last saw him.* Gordon's face was scruffy, as though he were beginning to grow a beard. He wore dirty sneakers, blue sweatpants, and a grey long-sleeve t-shirt with holes around the collar. Part of the collar was in his mouth, and the fabric around his mouth was dark, soaked with his saliva.

Mother stepped to Gordon and leaned down to put both of her arms around him. "Hello, dear," she whispered in his ear. Gordon stood still while Mother hugged him. It surprised Annie to see Mother hug him so close. She wondered if Mother had seen the wet area on his shirt. *Maybe she didn't feel his spit when she hugged him since he only comes to her shoulder, where her skin is covered by her shirt.* Annie knew, though, since she was Gordon's height, if she hugged him she risked feeling the drool on her neck. She held the garbage bag in front of her body as a shield.

Mother held Gordon at arm's length to look at him. He stared ahead with a blank expression. "You look good. Maybe a little pale." She stuck her finger through one of the wet holes near the collar of his shirt, causing Annie to wince. "I see you're still gnawing on your clothes."

Gordon continued to stare as though Mother was a ghost and he was looking through her. *He doesn't act as though he knows who we are,* Annie thought, remembering their visit in his bedroom at the group home.

"I've got to use your bathroom," Brad said. Annie pointed down the hall. On his way out of the room, Brad wrapped his lanky arms around Annie and picked her up in a huge bear hug. "Look at you, kiddo!" he exclaimed. Annie didn't know what he meant, but she beamed just the same. "You're not smoking, too, are you?" he asked.

Annie shook her head.

"Good," he replied.

Mother took Gordon by the hand and led him to Annie. Annie realized how much all three siblings resembled each other. Gordon shared the narrow face, the sharp nose, and the cleft chin Annie associated with Mother and Brad. But Mother was right about Gordon's skin coloring. He was much paler than they were. *He's pale because he's sick. It's the leukemia.*

"Gordon, this is my daughter Annie. The last time you saw her, she was only a little girl," Mother said.

Annie smiled and waved, even though he stood only a few feet from her. *Is he going to be upset I didn't hug him?* she wondered. He stared at her with a blank expression on his face. *He doesn't seem offended.*

Brad returned from the bathroom. "Do you have anything to drink?" he asked, stretching his arms above his head and running his fingers across the ceiling.

"In the fridge," Mother replied. "Do you need to go to the bathroom?" she asked Gordon, leading him to the bathroom. He didn't answer, but he followed without hesitation, walking on his tiptoes. *Is he the son Grandma Jo couldn't control? He's so small! He's so calm!*

Brad sat down on the couch with the bottle of flat pop Linda refused. Annie sat on the floor across from him, in front of the television. She set the garbage bag by her side.

"How're you doing, kid?" he asked. With one hand, he held the two-liter bottle up to his mouth and took a drink.

"Fine," Annie replied. With Brad there, she didn't feel nervous about having Gordon in her home.

"What grade are you in now?"

"I'll be a junior in the fall," Annie said, delighted at his interest.

"You planning on graduating?" he asked before taking another drink from the bottle.

Annie nodded.

"You got a boyfriend?"

Annie blushed. "Not right now," she responded. She preferred that answer to the alternative, *No, I never have; all the guys here are jerks.* Annie imagined Brad pummeling Cody for assuming she was pregnant and implying she'd have sex with someone other than her boyfriend. Brad would have punched Cody a good one right in the stomach, causing Cody's head of greasy black hair to fall forward.

"Annie?" Mother called from the bathroom. "Can you bring me a pair of Gordon's pajamas?"

Annie looked at Brad, expecting him to leap from the couch to retrieve Gordon's suitcase from his truck. Brad, understanding her expectation, shook his head. He pointed the two-liter bottle at the garbage bag on the floor. *Really?* Annie asked by raising her eyebrow. Brad nodded his head, bringing the bottle back up to his lips for a final swallow.

Annie's fingers struggled with the knot tied at the top of the big, black bag.

"Annie?" Mother called again.

"Coming," Annie hollered back. She tore open the side of the bag and rummaged through it until she found a faded pair of men's pajama pants. She couldn't find a matching shirt, so she grabbed a plain white t-shirt. She took the clothes into the bathroom. Gordon was standing in front of the toilet with his pants around his ankles. His shirt was still in his mouth. Mother was fastening one of the pairs of protective underwear around his hips.

"I'm sorry," Annie said, backing out of the doorway.

"Bring them here," Mother said. "It's okay."

Gordon's eyes were closed.

"I couldn't find a pajama set," Annie explained. She set the clothes on the counter by the sink and walked into her darkened bedroom. She flipped the light switch and pulled back the covers. Not knowing how well the diaper would work during the night and seeing all the saliva he produced by sucking on his shirt, she was glad he'd be sleeping on Linda's mattress and not hers.

Brad was leaning his head back against the couch with his eyes closed when Mother joined him and Annie in the living room after putting Gordon to bed.

"He about fell asleep on the toilet," Mother said, settling down on the other side of the couch. "Are you hungry? Did you get something to eat?"

"Yeah, hamburgers," he said, opening his eyes.

"How was he when you got there?" Mother asked, lighting a cigarette.

"Like he was here. They had everything loaded in the bag and had it sitting by the door when I got there. All I had to do was sign some papers. He got into my truck without any problem."

"How was he during the drive?"

"He wouldn't shut up, telling me all sorts of wild stories. Did you know he prefers to travel by motorcycle?"

Mother shot him a look and he laughed. "He was fine."

Annie found it odd to see Mother trying to have a serious conversation with Brad. In the past, their time together was spent with Mom picking at Brad and then defending herself when he retaliated by squeezing her thigh in a cow-bite with his large hand, poking her in the ribs, or sticking his finger, after he'd spit on it, in her ear. The only other time Annie had seen them talk with serious expressions was when Grandma Jo died and Brad tried to rouse Mother out of her depression to help him settle the estate.

"How'd the place look?" Mother asked, blowing smoke into the air.

"Like it did last time we were there. It smelled like cleaning chemicals, but it looked dirty."

"Well," Mother noted, "it doesn't look like he was being starved. He's got more meat on his bones than any of us."

The three of them sat in silence. Annie wondered if they'd talk about the abuse allegations. They didn't.

"Well, let me know if you need anything," Brad said, putting his hands on his knees to stand. Mother shot sparks of fire out her eyes, making her look like she was ready for a fight.

"You're leaving already?" Mother asked in an accusatory tone.

"Yeah, I've got some things to do tomorrow."

Annie was disappointed his visit was so brief. *He's not seen us in forever! Why is he so anxious to leave?* she wondered. *Is it to get away from this small town or is it to get away from us? Would he stay longer if I were more interesting to talk to?*

"We have things to do tomorrow, too," Mother snapped. But Annie knew Mother wouldn't try to stop him from leaving.

Annie stood and received the empty pop bottle. "Be careful," she said.

"Don't worry, kid. The night is still young." Annie hugged him goodbye and took the bottle to the kitchen.

Mother put her cigarette out and wrapped her arms around him. "Thank you for bringing him to us. I'll keep you posted on things."

As quickly as he had arrived, he left, leaving Annie and Mother standing in the living room looking at each other. "We might as well go to bed, too," Mother suggested. The night was still young for them, but Annie didn't argue.

She sneaked into her room to retrieve a night shirt and a pair of shorts from her dresser. On any other night, she wouldn't sleep with shorts on. But now there was a man living in the house, she figured she should cover herself, even if the man was retarded and wouldn't notice the difference if she weren't covered. Neither Mother nor Annie spoke as they brushed their teeth and washed their faces. Mom stood by the light switch in her bedroom, waiting for Annie to crawl into bed. Then she flipped the switch and made her way to her own mattress.

Mother and Annie each held their sheets under their chins like they were little kids. Their home felt different with Gordon sleeping across the hall.

"Did Gordon look like you remembered him?" Mother whispered.

"My memory of him was more from the picture in the kitchen than our visit. But he does look pale."

"Yeah," Mother agreed.

"Is he how you remembered him?" Annie whispered.

"Not at all," Mother replied.

They both stared at the ceiling, lit via the window by the streetlight outside. Just as Annie was about to close her eyes to go to sleep, she heard her mother say, "The apartment looks nice. You did a good job."

As she drifted off to sleep, Annie relished the compliment as though a piece of delicious, sweet cotton candy was melting on her tongue.

Chapter Seven

Mother and Gordon were deep asleep, their loud snores traveling down the hallway. As Annie brushed her teeth, she noticed Gordon's toothbrush was missing from the sink's toothbrush holder. *Mom must not have brushed his teeth,* she thought, spitting in the sink. *I wonder if there's even a toothbrush in his bag. I wonder if he has teeth.* She combed her wet hair. *Of course he has teeth. He chews on his shirt collar.* She flicked the loose hairs into the trashcan. *Since I don't have time to go to the dock before work, I might as well see what he brought with him.*

Grasping the black garbage bag at either side of the hole she'd torn the night before, she stretched her arms out wide, pulling the bag apart and dumping its contents onto the kitchen table. Then she shook the bag to make sure it was empty. Papers fluttered out and drifted down. Annie collected and shuffled them into an orderly pile. *I'll inspect them later.* She stored them on the seat of one of the chairs.

Annie gathered Gordon's clothing, pushing toiletry items

to the back of the heap. Gordon's clothes hadn't been folded and were crumpled. She tried to smooth each piece as she sorted the lot into like piles. Gordon had brought three pairs of sweatpants, in addition to the pair he wore last night. Though none of the sweatpants bore holes, they were worn thin and missing their fuzzy soft lining. She didn't find any shorts. *I hope the thin lining makes them more bearable to wear in the hot summer. That is, if he was allowed to go outside,* she thought.

Gordon had four small white undershirts, all yellowed in the armpits, two sweatshirts and five t-shirts, excluding the one he wore to bed. Like the sweatpants, the sweatshirts were worn thin. All the shirts had holes underneath the collar. *He must suck on his shirts a lot,* Annie figured, cringing at the thought. *Hey! None of these shirts are the ones we sent for Christmas!* Annie shook the garbage bag again, but she knew by feeling how light it was it was empty. *I'll have to tell Mom about this.*

The clothing inventory ended with Gordon's six pairs of mismatched socks and four pairs of stretched, discolored underwear. *If he has underwear, then he must be at least partially toilet trained,* Annie deduced. Gordon's initials, written in thick black marker, labeled each item of clothing on the tag or inside seam, except for the socks. The toes of the socks bore handwritten labels with a variety of initials. Annie wondered if family members of A.L. and S.C. were looking at socks with Gordon's initials written on the toes.

Assessing Gordon's lack of wardrobe, Annie realized she or Mother would be doing laundry every three days to keep him in clean clothes. *That won't work. I don't mind laundry, but I don't like it enough to do it every few days!* She retrieved a pen and small writing pad from the kitchen junk drawer and made a list of the things he needed. Then she stacked the folded items into one great pile and picked them up. They had a musty smell to them, so she held them away from her body as she crept down the hall and into her bedroom. *I'll wash these tonight if I have time.*

She set the clothes on the floor next to her dresser and pulled open the bottom drawer. The drawer was full of her nightshirts and flannel pants. She took the items on top of the dresser and placed them into the open drawer. The two items she handled with the most care were her jewelry box painted with bright red roses which Linda had looked at yesterday (without asking) and her snow-globe with the white cartoon figure holding a yellow star received from Grandma Jo. Annie pushed the drawer closed with her foot and separated Gordon's clothes into neat piles on the dresser's top.

As she started to leave, she noticed Gordon was awake, staring at her and sucking on his shirt collar.

"Good morning," she said.

He didn't respond in any way. *I'm not sure he can hear. Maybe Mom convinced herself he could hear because, with all his other problems, she didn't want to believe he's also deaf.* Annie waved and smiled, which were her best guesses of sign language for a happy hello.

"I'm Annie," she said, pointing to herself. "I'm your sister's (pointing to Mother's framed picture on the nightstand) daughter (pretending to rock a baby in her arms). You're (pointing at Gordon) staying with us (pointing to herself and then again to Mother's framed picture on the nightstand) until we can find you a new home (waving her hands to indicate the apartment)."

Is a new home going to upset him? He might have bad memories of his old one.

"A better group home," she corrected. Gordon continued to stare at her. He made no effort to sit up or to roll out of bed.

She started to move sideways toward the door, still facing him. "I'll (pointing to herself) see (pointing to her eyes) you (pointing to Gordon) this evening (pointing to the watch strapped to her wrist)." She exited the room, closing the door. She leaned against the wall and sighed. *That was a total failure. I guess I'll need to go to the library for a book on sign language-which will only help if he already knows sign language. Even if he does know it, I doubt he'll use it. All he does is stare at me!* She looked at her watch again. She needed to hurry to make it to work on time.

Annie returned to the kitchen to take inventory of the toiletry items on the table. Gordon had brought a small bottle of aftershave, an electric razor with whisker bits stuck to it, a toothbrush with bent bristles and dirty handle, a hair brush, and a rusty pair of nail clippers. Everything needed to be replaced. Annie added the toiletry items to her shopping list for Gordon. Then she picked up each item with the tips of her thumb and index finger and carried them one at a time into the bathroom. When she finished, she washed her hands and entered Mother's bedroom. She knelt next to Mother and tapped her shoulder.

"Wake up," she whispered.

Mother frowned but didn't open her eyes.

"I've got to go to work. Gordon's awake, but he's not out of bed."

"Gordon?" Mother asked, rubbing her eyes.

"Your brother, Gordon…remember? He's in my room."

"Oh, that's right," Mother said, propping herself up on her elbows and looking at the alarm clock next to the mattress on the floor.

Annie stood and stepped to the bedroom door. "I organized his clothes and put them on top of my dresser. I didn't see any of the clothes we sent him for Christmas, and he needs some new bathroom items. Do you want me to buy what he needs after work today?"

Mother nodded. "Come give me a kiss," she said.

Annie took a step back into the room, leaned over, and kissed her mom on the cheek. Mother lay back down and rolled over. Annie left the bedroom door open so Mother would be able to see Gordon if he left Annie's room. Back in the kitchen, she grabbed a fistful of money from the cookie jar and left the apartment, locking the door behind her.

"Crap!" Annie exclaimed, noticing the forgotten grocery cart in the parking lot. She gripped the cart's push bar and divided her journey to work between a brisk walk and a slow jog. It wasn't until she had her smock tied around her waist and the register open she realized she'd forgotten her journal and lunch at home. *Oh well, I work in a grocery store. I can always use some of the money from the cookie jar to buy something to eat,* she consoled herself. *And a new pad of paper.*

The day passed without excitement. Annie scratched her itch to write by writing descriptive phrases on the back of Gordon's shopping list. She was in the midst of trying to describe a copper penny lying on the grocery's brown tiled floor when Kelly Foster's dad came through the checkout line on his way home from work. He stood before Annie, tall and rigid. She pushed the list into her pocket and picked up the can of chicken noodle soup he'd placed on the conveyor belt. She scanned it and reached for the next item.

"You're the little girl from across the street, aren't you?" he said in a tone that sounded more like a statement than a question.

"Yes," Annie's throat screeched. Embarrassed, she touched her throat with her hand as if slight pressure would make it behave. "Yes, sir," she responded. She purposefully looked down at the box of crackers in her hand.

"Did you know Kelly has the chickenpox?"

Chickenpox? She glanced up and said, "No. Didn't she have them as a child?" She looked back down at the groceries.

"She had a mild case in pre-school, but apparently it wasn't strong enough to make her body immune. She's such a delicate child. I'm afraid she's going to be awfully ill. That disease is harder, the older you are."

Annie wouldn't have thought to describe Kelly as delicate. Flighty and bossy maybe, but not delicate.

"That's too bad," Annie said, trying her best to sound concerned. She even shook her head a few times while she scanned a tube of anti-itch ointment.

"I'm sure she'd enjoy knowing people are thinking about her. You could send her a get-well card."

Annie nodded, waiting for him to invite her to visit Kelly and cheer her up. But he didn't. So she smiled at him and handed him his change and stocked grocery bag.

After Mr. Foster exited the store, Angela arrived for her shift and opened the other checkout lane. Annie switched off her check-out light. After storing her smock under the register, she pulled Gordon's list back out of her pocket. Cody approached her. *Why can't he leave me alone for just one day?* she wondered.

Cody stared at her with an expression as dark as his dyed black hair.

"Yes?" she asked, feeling impatient.

"You seemed quite chatty with that man. Do you know him?"

"Not really," Annie replied. "Do you?"

Before she could ask why he even cared, he replied,
"Yeah, he's a real jerk of a neighbor."

Neighbor? Trying not to sound too interested, she asked, "Where do you live?"

"Two houses down from that guy, on the other side of the street. Why?"

Two houses down. Other side of the street. He lives in that abandoned-looking house! I had no idea people lived there. Well, that makes sense. He's the type of person to live there. "I live near him, too," Annie answered. She picked up a grocery basket and walked past him to begin collecting the items on her list.

"Where?" Cody asked, following her. "Where do you live?"

"In the apartments across the street from 'that guy.'"

Cody stopped walking as though he couldn't think and walk at the same time. He hurried to catch up to her. "Why don't

I ever see you out front there?" he demanded as they entered the hygiene aisle.

"Because I don't hang out on the street!" she snapped. *What kind of girl does he think I am?* "Why haven't I seen you outside?"

"Because that's my dad's house, and I live with my mom!" he countered with a raised voice matching hers.

Annie yanked a red toothbrush off the wall and tossed it in the basket. Surprised at her willingness to defend the father of the girl who ignored her in school, she asked, "Why do you think Mr. Foster's a jerk?" What she really wanted to ask was, *How can you, a total jerk, think anyone else is a jerk?* She took her time pushing her cart, not wanting to walk out of ear shot and miss his response.

"He came to the store once after he heard my grandpa was sick. Dying of cancer. He told me prayer could heal my grandpa. He said if I prayed God would save my grandpa just like God had saved his wife after her car wreck." Cody and Annie stopped in front of the electric razors.

"So?" Annie asked.

"I prayed."

"And?"

"He died," Cody muttered. He walked away, his shoulders slumped.

Annie stared at his back until he disappeared into his office. *That's the most civilized conversation we've ever had,* she realized. *Of course, he's still an angry bastard, but at least this time his anger was directed at someone else!* She focused her attention back on her shopping list.

Annie couldn't tell by reading the descriptions on the packages what kind of shaver Gordon needed. Besides, all the electric razors the store carried cost more money than she'd grabbed from the cookie jar. She decided to clean Gordon's old one. Before she left the healthcare aisle, she picked up a stick of deodorant that caught her eye. She hadn't put the item on her list because Gordon hadn't brought any with him. She reviewed the list for other missing items he might need. *Floss? He can use ours.* Having found all the items, she stood in line at Angela's checkout lane and made small talk with her while her items were totaled.

Imaging all the things that could go wrong with Gordon when she would be alone with him before Mother got home from work, Annie considered delaying her journey home. She thought about walking back to Cody's office to tell him Mr. Foster was only trying to help by encouraging Cody to pray. She could suggest Mr. Foster might have even changed since then, seeing how he'd bought ointment for Kelly's chickenpox instead of relying on a prayer chain to relieve her itch. But instead of walking to the back of the grocery store to seek out Cody, she walked out the grocery store's door. With a plastic bag in each hand, she put one foot in front of the other all the way home.

Chapter Eight

Linda sat on the couch, leaning forward, captivated by the television. Her frizzy grey hair was pulled up on the side of her head and held by a rubber band that was losing the battle of keeping the strays off her neck. Her jaw was busy working a piece of gum. Her hands clutched a large glass full of ice and, Annie would have bet, diet pop. Gordon sat at the far end of the couch, sucking on the collar of his shirt and looking at the television. Annie couldn't tell whether he was paying attention to the evening news program. The segment "A Day in the Life" was on, featuring a burly repossession man employed by a furniture store in the city.

"I just don't understand why anyone would buy something they couldn't pay for. Why would anyone want to live like that? It doesn't make sense!" Linda exclaimed, setting her glass on the coffee table and shaking her head so that more frizzy locks fell loose from the rubber band.

"Hello," Annie said, after determining Linda hadn't heard her enter and was either talking to herself or to Gordon.

Linda screamed and clutched her chest. “Oh! Ya startled me!” she gasped, breathing hard. She slumped over in her seat. Annie dropped the plastic grocery bag with Gordon’s toiletry items and took a step toward the couch. *Is she all right? Is she having a heart attack?* As Annie reached out her hand to touch Linda’s back, Linda popped up, having bent down to take a pack of gum from her purse. She held it out to Annie. “What a piece?”

“No, thank you,” Annie replied, exhaling a deep breath. She walked into the kitchen. “How did things go today?”

In response, Linda held a finger in the air, telling Annie to wait. She turned up the volume on the television. Annie opened the refrigerator to look for a snack. She hadn’t eaten any lunch.

“Another murder on the east side of the city,” Linda said, heaving her body off the couch and walking into the kitchen. “I’m so glad we live in a small town where nothing bad happens.”

Annie thought, *Something bad must have happened in this small town to make Cody so angry.* She took a thin slice of cheese from its package, folded and tore it into four pieces, and put one piece in her mouth.

“Things went just fine,” Linda answered. She swallowed the last of her diet pop, dumped the ice into the drain, and placed the empty glass in the sink. She reached for the phone, smacking her gum in synch with her fingers pushing the buttons. Annie noticed Linda’s glass was the only dirty dish in the sink.

“Gary? It’s me. I’m ready,” Linda said into the receiver before hanging it up. *Did you talk to him enough to know whether he’s been drinking?* Annie wanted to ask.

“Anyway,” Linda continued, “we got along just fine. We watched TV. One of the talk show programs was especially good! It was about wives who had secrets and needed the support of the audience to tell their husbands. I’d love to be an audience member and help people like that.”

Annie put another piece of cheese in her mouth to keep from speaking. Linda started to describe each of the wives' secrets. Annie swallowed the small pieces of cheese, hoping the food would soon hit her bloodstream. She was starting to feel irritated. She wanted Linda to tell her what to expect from Gordon and then leave. She had to instruct herself, *Annie, she's doing us a favor. So calm down and be thankful.*

In the midst of telling Annie about the third couple's shattered marriage, a truck horn sounded from the parking lot. Linda scurried to retrieve her purse.

"Anything I should know about?" Annie asked, pushing the last cheese segment into her mouth and following to hold the door open for Linda.

"Nothing much happened," Linda called out over her shoulder to Gordon, who continued to look at the television. "We just watched TV, didn't we, buddy?" Gordon didn't respond.

Linda hurried to the truck and held the handle as she waited for Gary to lean over the seat to unlock the passenger side.

"You're an angel!" Annie hollered, wanting to make sure Linda would be back tomorrow to stay with him.

Linda beamed as she rolled down the window. Annie heard her explaining to Gary, "I don't mean to lock the door and make you lean over the seat to unlock it. It's jus' habit." The truck rolled out onto the street.

Annie closed the front door and fished her key out of her pocket to lock it from the inside. She picked up the television remote from the couch, pointed it at the set, and turned down the volume. If she'd been home alone or with her mom, she would have switched the set off. But she opted to have a bit of background noise to make Gordon's silence less noticeable. Gordon continued to sit on the couch, but he was now staring at Annie. She stared at the blank expression on his face. *I wished he talked. I wish he could tell me why he stares like that. Like he's not human.*

The thought of improvising sign language to communicate with Gordon, like she'd tried that morning, appealed less to her than receiving a truck ride from a drunken Gary. If Mother thought Gordon could hear, then Annie would take her word. She walked over to Gordon and extended her hand like she'd seen Mother do last night. He took it and stood. *Thank goodness his hand is dry!* Annie had been right about his height, calculating she might be half an inch taller. She led Gordon to the kitchen table. He sat down in one of the chairs, staring up at her.

"Are you hungry for dinner?" No answer. "I thought I'd bake chicken and make macaroni and cheese." Silence. A jingle trying to entice people to buy baked hams played on the television.

After defrosting the chicken breasts in the microwave and sprinkling them with seasoned salt, Annie opened the preheated oven. A wave of heat hit her face. She jerked her head away in response and blindly placed the baking pan on the middle rack. Then she inspected the pot of water on the lit burner. Streams of bubbles cut through the water in the pot. Annie emptied the box of noodles into it and commenced setting the table. She felt Gordon's blank stare following her around the kitchen. She placed two glasses of water on the table. Gordon reached for his glass. Annie stirred the noodles, watching him. He drank all the water without stopping to take a breath.

Annie extended her open hand to him, and Gordon held the empty glass out to her. She took it and refilled it. With one breath, he again consumed the water. Anger bubbled up within Annie's chest as though she were the pot of boiling water. Her thoughts were scattered as though they were the noodles being tossed about by the boiling water. *There better not be… Linda better have…*Annie threw open the refrigerator door. The new two-liter of diet pop was nearly empty. Slamming the door, she looked into the sink at the lone dirty glass. *Where's Gordon's cup? She didn't offer him anything to drink! What's* *she thinking?* Without a satisfying answer, Annie finished cooking dinner. After filling Gordon's and her plates with food, she refilled his water glass for the third time. As he took it from her, he started to chant, "yup…yup…yup," making Annie smile. *At least he has enough water now.*

Gordon seemed happy with the meal before him. He picked up his spoon at the handle and proceeded to push macaroni noodles around his plate, managing to scoop a few. It wasn't until after he'd eaten half of his macaroni and cheese that it occurred to Annie he might not know how to cut food with a fork and knife. Intending to cut his chicken into bite-size pieces, she reached across the table. Gordon squawked like he was a large, riled parrot, grabbed the sides of his plate, and pulled it back to him. Annie dropped her utensils and put her hands back into her lap. She sat still, stunned at his reaction.

"I just want to cut the chicken for you so you can eat it," she explained. His response didn't change. He kept his hands on the plate. His expression wasn't blank anymore. His eyes were wide and dark.

Annie collected her knife and fork from the middle of the table and demonstrated how to cut her own chicken into pieces. She tilted her plate so he could see what she'd done. "I just want to help." She leaned over the table with her fork and knife in hand to reach his plate. Keeping his tight grip on his plate, he allowed her to cut his chicken. Before sitting back down, she slipped Gordon's knife and fork away from his plate and carried them across the table with her. *I don't want him to attack me if I do something wrong. He only uses his spoon anyway.*

Safely seated in her chair, she took a deep breath. His defensive reaction to her assistance had unsettled her, and his loud squawk scared her. "Gordon, I'm here to help you," she addressed the top of his head as he stared down at his plate, pushing pieces of chicken around with his spoon. He didn't respond. She finished her meal in silence, listening to the game show on the television in the living room. Gordon finished his meal in silence, too. No more "yup…yup…yups." But no more squawks either, for that matter. The situation had deescalated and Annie was offended by his reacting to her help in such an aggressive way. *I gave you three glasses of water when Linda didn't give you any! Isn't that enough to show you I'm friendly?*

Now angry, Annie rose from the table and busied herself with cleaning up the mess she'd made cooking dinner. She threw away the empty macaroni box and opened the cabinet drawer to replace the seasoned salt. Her movements were loud and heavy. She peaked over her shoulder at Gordon. He didn't seem to notice. *Just let it go, Annie.* She gave an exhaustive sigh and began making up a plate of leftovers for Mother, who would be hungry after work. She wrapped the plate with foil and set it in the refrigerator. Then she ran the dishwater in the sink. She took her time cleaning the baking pan and pot, Linda's cup, and her own dinner dishes. With trepidation, she approached Gordon for his empty glass, plate, and spoon. She held out her hands, hoping he'd present the dishes to her. He did.

With a drying rack full of clean, wet dishes, Annie wiped down the table and turned off the kitchen light. Hand in hand, she led Gordon from the kitchen back into the living room to sit on the couch. As she rounded the couch, she looked at the television. An entertainment news program was on. Annie rolled her eyes. *I bet Linda watches those trashy shows, too.* As Gordon began to sit down, Annie noticed a dark spot on the cushion where he'd been sitting earlier. She pulled Gordon's arm to stand him back up. She touched the spot. It was wet. *Was I wrong?* she wondered. *Had Linda given him a drink, which he spilled, and then washed the cup herself to remove evidence?*

Then Annie thought of another reason for the wet spot. As she turned Gordon around to look at his backside, she hoped her hunch was wrong. It wasn't. A dark line had formed on

Gordon's sweatpants above each thigh where his diaper had leaked. Annie's stomach hurt and she felt light in the head. *I just stuck my hand in his pee!* Holding her contaminated hand up in the air where it couldn't do harm, she pulled Gordon by the arm into the kitchen. She led him to the chair he sat on during dinner. It, too, was wet. *No use getting another seat wet.* She sat him down.

Even though she already knew what cleaning products they had, she searched the kitchen cabinet below the sink. *Surely we have industrial cleaner stronger than generic antibacterial spray.* They didn't. It took one spray and three long scrubbing sessions with hand soap for Annie to feel satisfied her hand was clean. While she scrubbed, she reasoned, *Since the couch was wet when I got home, he needed a diaper change while Linda was here. She didn't give him anything to drink and then she didn't change his diaper! What good is she doing us if she doesn't take care of him?*

Annie marched over to the refrigerator to look for Mother's work number, which was written on a piece of paper held by a magnet. In a huff, she dialed. She informed the receptionist who she was, who she needed, and that it was an emergency. Annie waited for her mom to be called off the line to take the call. She kept her eyes on Gordon, who remained seated. She watched him close his eyes and slump forward until he started to fall, which woke him up. He sat up, started to close his eyes, and began to slump forward again.

"Annie! What's wrong? Are you okay?" Mother asked in a panic.

"No!" Annie yelled. "Gordon's diaper leaked on the couch and the kitchen chair!"

Mother was silent. "Is that it?" she asked.

"I stuck my hand in the pee!" Annie shouted, frustrated her mom didn't understand the horror of the situation.

Mother laughed.

"Mom!" Annie shrieked. "It's not funny! It's gross!"

"Oh, honey," Mother consoled, trying to stop laughing.

"I'm sorry. I don't mean to laugh. It's just that I thought you or Gordon was hurt or something even worse than that. He is very sick, you know."

Annie tried to swallow her frustration. *I need to be a team player,* she reminded herself. "What…do…I…do?" Annie asked with as much patience she could muster. *Tell me you're going to come home and take care of it.*

"Give…him…a…bath…and…put…a…new…diaper…on…him," Mother replied, with just as much patience.

Annie didn't respond.

"Annie? Are you still there?"

In a low and serious voice, Annie said, "Mom, I can't change his diaper or give him a bath."

Mother paused. "Annie, I need for you to at least try to change his diaper. He can't keep sitting in something so wet and full it leaks."

"I can't, Mom," Annie whispered.

"Annie, please." Defeated, Annie agreed and hung up the phone. She knew her mom was right. His diaper needed changing, and, with reluctance, she figured she knew how to do it after seeing her mom do it last night. *All I have to do is stand him in front of the toilet, take off the old diaper, and then put on a new one.* She again held out her hand to Gordon, who yawned as he took it.

"Why are you so tired? You got plenty of sleep last night. I know. I heard you snoring." Gordon looked at her. His dark, wide-eyed look from dinner was gone, replaced by his usual blank stare.

"I guess you don't hold grudges," she said. She gave a deep sigh. "Let's go change your diaper."

She led him into the bathroom and stood him in front of the toilet. She retrieved a new diaper from the bag and placed it on the counter next to the sink. She then walked into her old bedroom and brought back a dry pair of pants. She didn't see the benefit of changing his shirt, guessing he'd chew on the dry one, making it wet, as well. She held up the diaper and the pants so Gordon could see them. His eyes were closed. She continued to hold them for a few seconds until he opened his eyes again. He stared without understanding.

Here goes. She decided she'd change his diaper standing at his side. That way, she was less likely to see his penis. She squatted down, grabbed his pants around his waistband, and pulled them down to his feet. He was very shaky, lifting each leg to step out of his pants. He held onto Annie's shoulder to steady himself. His shakiness was the second sign Annie had noticed indicating his illness. His pale skin had been the first.

After tearing the diaper's sticky tabs to unfasten it, Annie pulled the diaper down between his legs. It was heavy with urine. *How did you pee so much if you didn't have anything to drink?* she wondered. She tossed the diaper into the trashcan, where it landed with a thud. She then situated the dry diaper between his legs and brought it up to his waist. She pulled open the new sticky tabs and fastened the diaper on both sides. She never saw his penis, although she did see, by accident, his hairy butt. Trying to forget the visual, she held a pair of dry sweatpants so Gordon could step into them. Again, he held onto her shoulder to steady himself. She pulled up the clean pair of pants. *Finished!*

Annie wiped the sweat off her brow and saw Gordon rubbing his eyes with his hand, just like a baby does when it's tired. Having on a dry diaper didn't seem to matter to him. He gave no sign of appreciation for the uncomfortable work Annie performed. Instead, he yawned and closed his eyes. Shaking her head, she looked at her watch. It was shortly after nine o'clock.

"Want to go to bed?" she asked. She didn't wait for an answer. She led him into her bedroom. *Mom can brush his teeth in the morning,* she thought. Before she had time to flip on the overhead light, he had climbed into bed and pulled the cover up around him. He closed his eyes and rolled over onto his side with his back facing the door. Annie gathered the piles of his clothes from the dresser's top and pulled the door closed but for a small crack.

After throwing the clothes and detergent into the laundry basket, Annie retrieved the wet pants from the bathroom and proceeded outside to the apartment's separate laundry facility. While his clothes washed, she scrubbed the couch cushion and kitchen chair. By the time the clothes were in the dryer, she found the plastic bag of toiletry items she'd bought for Gordon still on the floor next to the door. She unpacked the new items and threw away those Gordon brought. She wetted a paper towel and wiped off Gordon's electric razor. She watched television until his clothes were dry, and then she went to bed. Both she and Gordon were sound asleep by the time Mother arrived home and sat down at the kitchen table to eat the leftover chicken and macaroni.

Chapter Nine

Annie woke early and crawled out of bed to sneak into her bedroom for a fresh change of clothes. Gordon was sleeping curled into a little ball with the sheet crumpled at the foot of the bed. For once, the collar on his shirt was dry. Annie resisted the impulse to pull the sheet up around his shoulders. She didn't want to wake him, startle him, and hear him squawk at her. *Heaven forbid I try to do something nice for him again. I can just see him waking up and thinking I'm taking his sheet instead of covering him up.*

She showered and dressed. During the summer months she let her hair dry in the sun as she walked to the dock to sit on the steps overlooking the river. In the winter months, she took her showers at night and let her hair dry as she slept. She had ignored Kelly's pearl of advice suggesting Annie visit a salon for a stylish cut maintained with a bit of gel. Although as Annie studied herself in the steam-free splotches on the bathroom mirror, she wondered whether her response to Brad's question about a boyfriend would have been different if she did put more time into her appearance.

Kelly makes life seem so easy. Wear trendy clothes and wear my hair a certain way and I'll have unlimited friends and boyfriends. With friends and boyfriends, my life will be all happy. But friends and boyfriends won't bring Grandma Jo back to life or have Brad move back home. Annie turned from the mirror and busied herself by hanging her towel from the plastic rack above the toilet. Then she entered the kitchen and started a pot of coffee.

She was sitting at the table, looking out the window and peeling a banana for her breakfast when Mother wandered out of the bedroom, pulling her robe closed around her. "He still asleep?" Mother asked, pointing at Annie's bedroom door.

"He was 30 minutes ago. What are you doing up?"

Mother sat on the kitchen chair Gordon's diaper had leaked on during dinner. Annie knew it was clean, though she still felt an urge to encourage Mother to take a different chair. Before she could, Mother continued, "I wanted to talk to you about what happened last night with his diaper. I know it must have been tough on you."

The aroma of freshly brewed coffee filled the air. Annie chewed the bite of banana in her mouth. After swallowing, she said, "I changed his diaper, but I didn't give him a bath."

Mother nodded as though she had expected as much. "Did he cooperate?"

"Yes. But he got mad at me during dinner and squawked at me."

Mother frowned. "What happened?" She started to rise from her seat, looking at the pot of coffee. Annie motioned her to sit back down, she'd bring her a cup. As she reached into the cabinet for a mug, Annie explained about cooking dinner, noticing Gordon wasn't cutting his meat, and trying to help.

"You know," Annie said, setting a cup of black coffee in front of Mother, "he looks normal, except for his stare. I know he's disabled, but I can't tell by looking at him what he can and can't do. He doesn't do what I think he should be doing so I try to help, which makes him mad."

"Maybe his reaction had nothing to do with you. Maybe he's just used to people trying to take his food."

"I hadn't thought of that," Annie replied, biting off another piece of banana.

"The stare is part of the autism," Mother commented, blowing on the surface of the coffee in her mug. "But there are moments when his eyes change and you can see the person trapped inside, or at least, that's how I look at it. He'll relax when he has a routine here. All the change must bother him."

"How can you tell he's bothered?" Annie asked, stirring a spoonful of sugar into her own coffee. "Other than when he got mad at me, he's been like a zombie! Even after he was done being mad, he went back to being a zombie!"

"How he's been here is not how he normally acts," Mother replied. "I bet they drugged him to keep him calm until we got him home. He didn't bring any medication with him, did he?"

Annie shook her head. She hadn't found any medication in the garbage bag.

"That's what I thought. I called Brad last night to give him an update, and he said he found Gordon's binder with all his medical history pushed up under the seat of his truck. But no medicine. However, that binder should tell us what he's supposed to be taking."

"Do we need to take him to the doctor?"

"Let's wait for the binder."

"Is Brad going to bring it?" Annie asked, hoping for another visit.

"No, he's going to mail it. We should get it in a couple of days."

Annie poured Mother more coffee, trying to hide her disappointment. Mother found her purse hanging on the back of another chair and searched it until she found a cigarette.

"So, what else happened?" Mother asked, lighting up and waving her hand in the air to clear the smoke.

Annie shared her concerns about Linda not giving Gordon anything to drink or changing his diaper. She continued, "I could see her not wanting to change his diaper. I didn't even want to do that. But I don't think she even realized it needed changing!"

Mother looked concerned. She sipped her coffee, swallowing Annie's news along with the hot dark liquid. "Is there anyone else who could help us?" Annie asked.

"She wasn't my first choice," Mother clarified. "I tried a couple of other people…some of the stay-at-home wives of the men at the plant. But Gordon being an adult with a disability scared them off. One wife suggested I look into an adult day center in the city. But I'd have to pay the center and drive all that way. Linda's our best bet." She took a long drag on her cigarette. "I'm hopeful she'll work out. She used to work at the nursing home…you know, the one on Main Street across the railroad tracks and by the Goodwill." Annie nodded. Mother continued, "She has experience taking care of people."

"Why doesn't she work there any more?" Annie asked, wishing she had chocolate chip cookies to dip in her coffee, her favorite treat.

"I thought she quit because of her back. I hope that's why. You don't think she did anything to mistreat him, do you?" Mother asked.

"She just neglected him," Annie responded. Hearing herself say the words, she felt a pang of discomfort in her stomach. *It's true,* she insisted, wanting the feeling to go away. *Okay, maybe the word "neglect" is too harsh. Or maybe it isn't the right word. Children are neglected. Can adults be neglected, too?* The discomfort in her stomach persisted. *I didn't do anything wrong! Linda's the one who messed up!* Annie didn't want to tell Mother about her stomach ache. *When I'm at work I'll try to figure this stomach thing out.*

Mother interrupted Annie's thoughts by asking, "You'll be off work tomorrow, right?"

Annie nodded, thankful for the distraction.

"And I'll be off work on Thursday. Can I tell Linda to call you at work if she needs anything?"

Annie didn't like the thought of being the emergency contact. "I'm not sure I'll have any idea of what to do if something goes wrong."

Mother nodded. "How about she calls you first. If you need help, then call me and I'll come home."

"Okay," Annie agreed, drinking the last of her coffee. "I can do that."

"I'll call the state again today to see what progress has been made on finding a new group home." Mother put out her cigarette in an ashtray.

Annie glanced at her watch. "I better get going," she said.

Mother drank the last of her coffee. "Is there enough for another cup?"

"Yes," Annie said, picking her journal up off the table. "Shoot! I need to make my lunch!" She hurried to the refrigerator. She put some meat in between two pieces of bread and wrapped the sandwich in plastic. There was no time to add mustard. *I've never thought meat and bread were dry before. If Linda has jinxed me with her condiment need, I'm going to be mad!* She tore a banana off the bunch before rushing to the door. *A drink! No time. I'll buy one from the machine outside the store*, she decided, not wanting to re-cross the 10 feet it'd take to return to the kitchen.

Mother followed Annie to the door. "What did you do with the clothes Gordon wore last night?"

"I washed them. I washed all his clothes. They smelled," she said, wrinkling her nose. "They're in piles on top of the dresser."

"What a good girl you are." Mother kissed Annie on the cheek.

For the second day in a row, Annie found herself dividing her commute to work between jogging and race-walking. *At least I don't have to push that cart this time.* By the time she had her lane open and her smock pulled over her head and tied at the waist, she was out of breath and had to sit on her stool with her hands on her hips for a few minutes. Always being skinny without having to exercise, it took times like this to remind her being skinny didn't mean she was in shape.

During her downtime between customers, Annie examined the pain she felt in her stomach when she accused Linda of being neglectful. The feeling had made her want to yell in anger. Yet her mouth remained closed. The feeling haunted her, to her surprise. She held no preconceived notions about Linda that came close to matching the intense sensation in her stomach. *I hope the feeling goes away as quickly as it arrived,* she wished, closing her pencil in her journal to wait on a customer whose grocery cart was full of ice-cream treats.

Failing to diagnose her stomach ailment, Annie tried to capture Gordon's blank gaze with words in her journal. His expression made her think of a deep stone well in the middle of the country, dividing a dense forest speckled with the brilliant colors of blue jays and cardinals and a rolling bright green field speckled with purple, yellow, and orange wildflowers. The forest and field were united by a royal blue sky filled with white fluffy clouds. Looking into Gordon's eyes was like leaning over the side of a well full of water. But no matter how she strained her eyes to see or her ears to hear, she neither saw the ripples nor heard the plunks of the pebbles she tossed into it.

It wasn't until after the lunch rush Annie found time to eat her sandwich. She bit down into her ham sandwich, and, before she began chewing, determined the meat and bread were dry. *That darn Linda!* She set the sandwich down on the plastic wrap and searched for two quarters in her pocket. She looked up and down the empty aisles to make sure a customer wasn't approaching. She locked her register and exited the store to buy a pop. She was punching the selection button on the machine outside when Cody approached from the parking lot. He was stuffing his keys into his pants pocket with one hand and trying to straighten his tie with the other.

"You have your own car?" Annie asked, retrieving the can from the machine.

"Yup," Cody replied, reminding Annie of Gordon's happy chant. Cody pointed at a small blue car parked at the far end of the parking lot. Annie didn't know much about cars, including makes and models. She couldn't tell whether he had a good car. It looked old, with a dent in the back driver's side door and rust spots on the frame over the tires. "You drive?" he asked.

"No. I'm still fifteen. I'll take driver's ed this fall. I have a late birthday."

Cody and Annie walked to the door. He paused for Annie to enter first. Annie was busy thinking about whether to ask him how much he'd paid for his car. She wanted to know how much money she needed to save to buy herself a car. *Think of all the places I could drive to gain inspiration for my writing... parks filled with deer and birds...restaurants filled with friends and family laughing while eating, and cafes filled with lovers meeting for drinks...Oh, the things I could write about!* Sensing Cody was in as good a mood as he could be, since he didn't get onto her about being outside instead of at her station, Annie continued the conversation.

"Did your family buy it for you?" She picked up her sandwich to take another bite. She acted as though she wasn't that interested in his response. If he thought her eager, he might not respond.

"No, I bought it myself." He stood in front of her lane, staring at her. She expected him to continue talking, but he didn't. He stared at her, and she stared at him. She didn't know what to say. The silence started to feel awkward. She took another bite of her sandwich. He cleared his throat. "I'm sorry about calling that guy a jerk yesterday."

To keep herself from spitting out the partially chewed food,

Annie covered her mouth with her hand. She laughed. Cody glared at her and walked away.

"No, wait," Annie said, calming herself and swallowing her food. Cody waited with his back to her. "It's just that, with all the crappy things you've said to me, you apologize for that insignificant thing!" she explained.

"What crappy things?" Cody asked, spinning around. He sounded annoyed. Annie questioned why, only a moment ago, she thought he was in a good mood. But she wasn't going to back down.

"Well, for one, calling me a whore with the whole 'it doesn't take a boyfriend to get pregnant' comment." She felt good confronting him. The painful feeling in her stomach lessened.

"That's not what I meant," Cody said without apology. Annie wasn't satisfied.

"What else could it have meant?" she demanded.

"It just came out wrong."

A young woman with a crying toddler sitting in the front of the grocery cart entered Annie's aisle and began removing items from the cart. There were dark circles under the woman's eyes. She ignored her crying baby and hoisted her purse strap back up on her shoulder, which fell again when she leaned into the cart to grab her groceries. The woman looked only a few years older than Annie. *Sometimes not having a boyfriend is a silent blessing.*

"Seriously," Cody said. "Sorry." This time he sounded like he meant it. He walked back to the manager's office.

As he left, every rude comment he'd ever made during her employment at the grocery store leapt to Annie's mind. She opened her mouth to call out to him to have him return, but she was no match against the wailing baby. She closed her mouth and scanned a container of baby wipes. She felt powerful having him apologize, and she wanted more from him. She considered following him into his office after she was done checking the groceries to force an apology for every wrong he'd committed against her. She wanted to hear him tell her he hadn't been a fair boss and he thought she deserved better.

"Annie, you have a telephone call," sounded over the store's intercom. *Oh no.* Her heartbeat matched the intensity of the pain growing in her stomach. She totaled the cost of the woman's groceries and loaded them into bags. She considered delaying the phone call by helping the tired woman to her car, but she decided against it. After completing the sale, she made her way to the manager's office, looking at her watch. *Calm down. Linda's only been alone with him for 30 minutes. That's not enough time for something to go wrong. She probably wants me to pick up some more diet pop. Maybe it's not even Linda on the phone in the first place. Maybe Ms. Erwin is calling about my revised poem.*

Yet as she brought the phone to her ear, she expected to hear Linda's voice on the line. She was right.

"Annie, come home! I can't handle him!" Linda yelled, panicked.

"Linda, calm down."

Linda didn't calm down. Words poured from her mouth. "He took my cup of pop and started to drink it! When I told him to stop, he threw it at me!"

Is that all? Annie thought. *Is this how Mom felt last night when I called about the leaky diaper?*

Linda continued speaking at a rapid pace, "He keeps running for the door! I don't have a key to lock it, and I can barely keep him inside. I had to move something in front of it to block him! Wait, he's trying to go outside again!"

With a bang that hurt her ear, Annie heard the phone drop onto the kitchen counter. She heard Linda yell, "No, you have to stay inside!" Then she heard Linda yell, "No! No! No!"

But it wasn't until she heard Gordon squawk that Annie hung up the phone.

"I have to go," she said to Cody, who had entered his office. She took off her smock and tossed it onto a chair in his office. She didn't even turn off her checkout lane's light or take time to grab her journal before she left. She ran as fast as she could, all the way home.

Chapter Ten

Annie took one stride to protect Linda from Gordon and the next to protect Gordon from Linda. *If only I knew why he squawked,* her mind raced. *Was she just trying to help him, like I was last night, cutting his chicken? Did she upset him without meaning to? Did she drink in front of him without offering him something? Or did she do something to hurt him or scare him?* A train passed below as Annie ran across the bridge over the railroad tracks. She wished she could travel as fast, especially when she saw Gary's truck parked along the street outside the apartment complex. *Oh, God,* Annie thought more than prayed. *What if Gary's drunk? What happens if he forgets Gordon's sick and not even strong enough to hurt Linda?* All of Annie's strides became those to help protect Gordon.

As she reached the edge of the apartment's parking lot, the door flew open in unison with a loud squawk. Gordon hobbled outside in his socks, his big toe on his right foot poking through a hole. *Oh, he's trying to run,* Annie thought, watching him bend one leg and then swing the straight leg around in front. *I don't think there's anything wrong with his leg. Maybe the rocks hurt the bottom of his feet?* Gordon looked to his left and his right, as though he wanted to go somewhere but didn't know where. He squawked again.

"Gordon!" Annie called, changing her direction a bit to run to him. *Please don't run into the street*, she pleaded. *Just stay where you are. Just stand still!*

Linda appeared in the doorway and staggered outside. The front of her pale yellow t-shirt was wet and discolored, and it clung to her body. "Gordon! You get back here!" she hollered, her grey frizzy hair a mess. Gary appeared in the doorway with a cigarette hanging out of his mouth. He held up his wrist to look at his watch, indicating to Annie he was merely a spectator to the scene unfolding before them. Yet Annie didn't relax or slow her pace.

By this time, Gordon had seen Annie and started to move to her in a wobbly run. He reached out his hand, and as she reached him she took it in hers. She noticed, but didn't mind, that it was wet. She stopped running and leaned forward with her free hand on her knee to catch her breath. Relief rushed over her.

Linda met them and reached out her arm as if to grab Gordon and pull him back into the apartment. Annie straightened her body and stepped in front of Gordon so she was between him and Linda. "I have him, Linda," she said. Then, to avoid being offensive, she added, "It seems like you've been through a lot today. Why don't you rest a minute?"

But Linda wasn't ready to rest. "Yes, I have been through a lot!" she screamed. Annie watched Linda's hands curl into fists.

"Your mama didn't warn me about how he was acting today! The decent thing to do would have been to tell me. I could've had Gary stay with me! But he left, and I had to wait until he got all the way home to reach him by phone to tell him to come back! Your mama did this on purpose!" Linda's chest heaved with each short breath she took.

It was difficult for Annie to resist yelling back at Linda. *She has no right to accuse Mom of being mean on purpose!* But Annie managed to control herself better than Linda. Even though Linda's fists were clenched, her tone angry, and her words aggressive, Annie recognized something in Linda's presence she had experienced the night before during dinner. Linda was scared. Gordon might have scared her and hurt her feelings. *But it's easier to be angry. Reacting to Linda's anger won't help anything,* Annie told herself. Yet she continued to stand in front of Gordon.

"Linda," Annie soothed, "Mom cares too much about you to keep information from you. She'd never set you up. Plus, she knows you're an experienced care-giver." *Or at least we hope you are. Desperate times call for desperate measures.* Annie waited for Linda's response.

With her hands still clenched into fists, Linda chewed on Annie's words along with the bubblegum in her mouth. After blowing several bubbles out of habit, Linda's hands relaxed and her anger popped. "Well," she said, "your mama does know I have experience caring for people. And it doesn't seem like something she would do, trying to set me up."

Annie nodded. Hoping Linda was under control, Annie began to worry about Gordon. She felt him rocking behind her. *He's still upset. He might not even know what's going on.* She guessed he was on his tiptoes. She glanced at the ground behind her to see she was right.

Linda shook her head of frizz as though she were shaking the negative thoughts about Annie's mother from her head. "Whew!" Linda exclaimed, though she still looked worn out. She peered back at the apartment. "Oh, Gary!" she exclaimed. Gary was sitting on the concrete step in front of the door with his elbows on his knees. His cigarette still hung in his mouth. Linda's upper body swelled, and she looked at him with a grand smile as though he were the noble captain of a ship who had just saved her from drowning. He didn't return her smile, but he did raise his eyebrows as if to say, *What?*

Addressing Annie, Linda said, "I don't want Gary to have to make another trip into town in a couple of hours just to pick me up. So, I'm going to go ahead and go with him."

Annie nodded again, grateful Linda was leaving but concerned she was still upset. Despite her blowing bubbles and acting like she was better, she just didn't seem right to Annie. Linda stepped past Gary into the apartment. Gary rose and strode to his truck, flicking his cigarette butt into the street. Annie remained alert to everyone's movement, as though she were stationed as the lookout on Gary's ship. She wanted to be able to forestall any further danger. She held her body rigid, not wanting any movement on her part to disrupt the peace. Linda emerged from the apartment with her purse strap around her shoulder and a full glass of pop in her hand.

"Can I bring this back to you later?" she asked, holding up her plastic pink cup.

"That's fine," Annie said, forcing a smile. *Just leave,* she thought.

Linda walked across the small front yard to the truck parked in the street. She opened the door, plopped herself into the passenger seat, and swung the door shut. Annie relaxed, knowing there was now a sheet of metal, in addition to Annie's body, between Linda and Gordon. She watched Linda bite the rim of the pink cup to hold it as she used both hands to fasten her seatbelt. Annie was right not to expect Linda to wave good-bye as the truck rolled down the street. When the truck turned and disappeared from their sight, the telephone rang inside the apartment.

"Let's go inside," Annie said to Gordon. "The phone's ringing." She took a step, still holding his hand. She gently pulled him in the direction of the door, but he held his ground, continuing to rock. Annie counted the telephone rings as she waited for Gordon to take a step to her. She didn't want to hurry him and upset him. Three…four…five…On the sixth ring, he took a step on his tiptoes. Annie took another step to stay in front of him. He followed her. By the tenth ring, they were both inside the apartment. Annie dropped Gordon's hand, pushed the door closed, and ran to the phone. He began rocking again, swaying his weight from one foot to the other. It was Mother on the phone.

"Annie, what happened? I was handed a horrible message the receptionist said was from Linda!"

"Gordon threw her glass of pop at her. She thought you set her up by not telling her he was acting up today."

"Let me talk to her."

"She just left. Gary came and got her."

"But she was only there for an hour!" Mother exclaimed.

"I know. I didn't ask her what all happened. She was so upset I just wanted her to leave before either she or Gordon made things worse." Annie glanced at Gordon, who was still rocking. She wished she had taken the time to lock the door.

"What about your work?" Mother asked.

"I left." Annie took a seat on a kitchen chair facing Gordon, watching him stare at an invisible point in front of her.

"What's he doing now?" Mother asked.

"He's standing and rocking, but he's not squawking."

"The rocking is something he does to self-stimulate."

"What does that mean?" Annie asked, wrinkling her nose. She prepared to hear Mother say he was doing something sexual.

Mother paused, causing Annie more discomfort. "You know, I don't know. That's just what the doctors told Mom and me when he rocked at his appointments. I don't think either of us asked what it meant. We didn't want to look stupid. I think it's something to calm him down." Again, Mother paused. Then she asked, "Should I come home?"

Annie wanted to say, *Yes*. But she thought, *She's counting on me to help, and he seems okay right now. I can at least give it a try. I know the plant frowns on people taking off early, even for emergencies, because it leaves a gap in the line.*

"No," Annie replied. "We'll be okay."

"You sure?"

No, Annie thought, but she answered in the affirmative and hung up the phone. She put her head down into her open hands. *What in the world am I going to do now? It's too early to fix dinner. I don't know what to do to entertain him.* She looked up and watched him rock. She caught herself swaying in her chair in synch with his movement. *He's not hurting himself standing there. Maybe he'll rock all afternoon and evening. Maybe he'll wear himself out and go straight to bed.* Annie leaned back and put her feet up in the kitchen chair to her right. She was willing to spend the next two hours watching him rock. Her feet crumpled the papers on the chair's seat.

She reached under the table to pull the papers out. *With my luck today, those are unpaid bills never even taken out of their envelopes.* But she could tell by their feel the papers weren't bills. The papers were pieces of construction paper. *These are the papers from Gordon's garbage bag,* she remembered. She spread them out to look at them. Each paper bore a large, solid circle in the center with smaller solid circles around it. Each circle had a thick border. Annie peered at the circles before her. They had been drawn and colored by hand. She ran her fingers over the circles and felt the wax build-up from the crayons.

"Gordon," Annie called out. "Come here."

Gordon continued to stand, rocking back and forth staring at an invisible point between him and her and sucking on his shirt collar. Annie stood and approached him with one of the pictures in her hand. "Gordon," she said, putting her hand on his shoulder to keep him still. She waved the paper in the air to grab his attention. His stare transferred from the invisible point to the paper before him. He reached out and turned it around. *I was holding it upside down*, Annie thought.

She returned to the table and shuffled the other construction papers together. She carried the pile with her as she took Gordon's hand and walked into the living room. They sat on the couch, on the two cushions he hadn't peed on. Annie handed him the pile. With care, he took them in his hands, holding the drawing so she could look at it with him. In its center was a royal blue circle with a forest green border. Smaller yellow circles with red borders formed a frame of sorts around the blue circle. There was one tiny black circle with a brown border at the bottom in the center.

He's sharing his art with me, Annie realized. *But unlike me when I share my poems, he doesn't seem nervous.* She cleared her throat. "I like it," she said. "I like that shade of blue. It reminds me of a sky filled with white fluffy clouds."

Gordon dropped his shirt collar out of his mouth and chanted, "Yup…yup…yup." He moved the picture to the back of the pile and showed Annie a new picture featuring a large orange circle with a thick brown border. Together, they looked at each picture. Annie offered a positive comment on each one. Every few pictures Gordon turned the page so the picture's orientation was correct. Annie determined each picture had a smaller circle in the bottom center. *I won't hold his pictures upside down anymore.*

Annie had an idea. "Gordon, would you like to color some more pictures? We can go to the store and buy some paper and crayons." *Plus I can explain to Cody why I had to leave so abruptly.*

Gordon didn't respond to her voice. He continued to look at his artwork. Annie walked into her bedroom to retrieve the pair of dirty sneakers he had worn to their home. She held them away from her body so she wouldn't smell their foul odor as she brought them into the living room. She knelt down on the floor before Gordon and tried not to breathe as she put his shoes on his feet. He picked up each foot and allowed Annie to guide it into the appropriate shoe. She held her hands out to him to receive his drawings. After counting 60 seconds, she tapped the top of the pictures to get Gordon's attention.

"Let's go for a walk," she said smiling, pointing to the door.

Gordon set the pictures on the couch cushion beside him. He took Annie's hand, and this time, to Annie's relief, it was dry. *I never washed my hand from earlier when his was wet. I'll have to do that when we get back.* Also to Annie's relief, he waited by her side as she locked the door outside. Hand in hand, they walked, Gordon on his tiptoes, looking straight ahead as though he already knew the way.

Annie looked at him out of the corner of her eye. *I wish he weren't wearing a shirt with spit and holes on it, and I wish his hair wasn't messed up. And Mom still hasn't shaved his face. She needs to do that!* Annie sighed. *I can't imagine what people are going to think. He almost looks like a man brought up in the wild. If his beard were any longer, he'd look like a caveman. But maybe his looking crazy will make Cody believe I really did have an emergency at home and had to leave.*

At the store, Annie had to coax Gordon to enter as he was startled by the door automatically opening from their stepping on the black, plastic mat. By the time they'd reached the tiled floor, they had Angela's full attention. Angela held some change above a small boy's outstretched hand, a candy bar in his other. The look of anxiety on the boy's face indicated his worry over whether he'd ever receive his change. Angela's eyes were as big as the quarters in her hand. Leading Gordon, Annie raised her chin as she walked past Angela and through the store to the manager's office.

Cody was sitting at the computer pecking on the keyboard with his two index fingers.

"Didn't you take typing in school?" Annie asked.

Cody continued to look at the computer screen. "You come to finish your shift?"

"No," Annie replied. She pulled Gordon's arm so he had to take a step forward. He stumbled, trying to catch his balance and remain on his tiptoes. "This," she said a bit too loud, "is my uncle. He had a problem with his sitter, so I had to go home. The sitter left, so I need to stay with him today."

"Then why are you here?" Cody asked, still pecking at the keys. "Do you want my permission to go back home?"

No matter how many times I tell myself he can't get nastier, he does, she thought, angry he could still surprise her. She took a deep breath, trying for the second time that day to keep from responding to someone's negative energy. "I came to tell you what happened. In case you were worried." As soon as the words left her mouth, she wished she could take them back. *He wouldn't worry about me. I know that.* She added, "I mean, I thought I owed you an explanation for running out earlier."

Gordon started to pull on Annie's arm. Still holding onto his hand, she shook her arm. "Stop, Gordon!" she whispered to him.

Cody stopped pecking at the keyboard. He glanced at Gordon before meeting Annie's gaze.

"I guess you did owe an explanation to your co-workers, the people who had to step up to cover for you. I'll be sure to tell them. But don't expect them to thank you for your explanation."

"Why are you such a jerk?" she asked, not able to contain a calm composure.

Cody stood from behind his desk. "Watch it now. I am your manager."

For the second time, Gordon pulled on Annie's arm. As he did, she noticed her journal sitting on the far side of Cody's desk. She dropped Gordon's hand and reached for the book.

"This is mine," she snapped, grabbing it. "What's it doing here?" she demanded.

"You left it when you ran out on your shift," he replied, his voice steady.

"Did you read it?" Annie asked, her voice quivering. The look on Cody's face told her he had. Tears welled up in her eyes. Cody, who took delight in being mean to her, who insulted her any time he got the chance, had read her private poems. Her poems were her diary, a recording of the things she saw and the feelings she experienced. She clutched the book and held it close to her chest. She wanted to hit Cody with it. She wanted to hurt him. She wanted to make him feel vulnerable like she did now.

"You pathetic waste!" she spit out. "You had no right!"

Cody looked past her into the store and said, "You're going to buy that, I hope."

"What?" Annie asked, confused. "I'm not going to buy my own journal!"

"No," Cody said, starting to walk around his desk to the door. "Your … uncle."

Annie looked to her side. Gordon was gone.

Chapter Eleven

In front of cups of yogurt, cottage cheese containers, and milk cartons Gordon sat on the floor with his legs crossed. His hands grasped a pint of milk. *He's smart enough to figure out how to open the display doors,* Annie thought. *I've underestimated him.* She watched him try to gnaw off the lid. Luckily, he was hidden from the other shoppers by a tall display of processed cheese. It was the first time, in all her months of scanning boxes of cheese that didn't need to be refrigerated, Annie felt appreciation for the item.

"Don't you give him anything to drink?" Cody asked, reminding Annie he was standing beside her.

"Shut up," Annie muttered. "Just go away. I can handle this myself."

"I can tell."

Annie ignored the comment and knelt on the tiled floor next to Gordon.

"Gordon, please give me the bottle of milk," she requested,

forcing a smile. She reached out her hand, thinking, *Please don't make a scene.*

Gordon stared at her. He kept the bottle in his mouth, but he stopped biting the top. Annie continued to smile and wiggled the fingers of her outstretched hand. "Let's go pay for it. You can drink it when we're outside…on our way home."

Tucking her journal under her arm, Annie stood and extended both hands to Gordon. He started to take one of her hands when he looked over at Cody and stopped. Cody was walking to them.

Facing Cody, Annie snapped, "You just stay back! I don't need you hurting him, too." She turned her attention back to Gordon and said, "It's okay."

Keeping his eyes on Cody, Gordon took one of Annie's hands and stood. But then he dropped Annie's hand and began walking away from her. She followed, trying to stay close enough to be able to stop him from grabbing something else off the shelf but far enough away he didn't feel she was rushing at him. *How do I get control of him without upsetting him?* her mind raced. *I don't want him to squawk!*

Cody followed Annie, letting her set the pace. "I have the right to observe you two for security reasons," he said.

"Give it up, Cody," Annie muttered out the side of her mouth. "We're not going to steal anything."

Cody continued to follow them, unrelenting in his managerial duties.

Annie's feeling of helplessness grew, but she didn't want either Gordon or Cody to know it. *I'll give a little and then maybe he'll give a little. If I give Gordon some time to explore the store, then when I tell him it's time to go, he'll listen to me,* she planned, trying to ignore the tiny voice in the back of her head telling her that her plan was not a plan at all. Annie followed Gordon as he walked on his tiptoes up and down the aisles. Cody still followed Annie. Gordon held his pint of milk close to his chest, although he didn't put it back into his mouth. Instead, he sucked on the collar of his shirt. When they entered the cereal aisle with a portion dedicated to school supplies, Gordon dropped his pint of milk and hobbled straight-legged in the direction of the crayons.

"Yup…yup…yup," Annie heard him chant as she swooped down to pick up the plastic pint of milk rolling down the aisle. She straightened her body and looked to the sky. *Thank you for the chant, a sign that he's happy.* Annie joined Gordon's side. He held a box of crayons in his hands.

"You want to get some crayons?" she asked. Ignoring her, Gordon continued his mantra and tried to open the box. Annie envisioned the crayons spilling and rolling in all directions. *I was able to scoop up a rolling pint of milk. I can't do the same for 64 crayons.* She put her hands over the box and pried Gordon's fingers out from under the lid. In doing so, she tore the top of the crayon carton.

"No, Gordon! You have to wait until you get home to use them!"

Gordon struggled to free his hands from hers to pry open the lid of the box.

"No, Gordon!" Annie repeated.

Gordon gave a loud, shrill squawk. Annie winced at the noise. She imagined all movement in the grocery store stopping. Gordon abandoned the box in Annie's hands and reached for another box of crayons on the shelf.

"No, Gordon! Leave them alone! You have your box right here." Annie yelled even louder than his squawk. She was panicked. Things were spinning out of control. Cody approached tentatively and reached out his hand to Gordon.

"Get back, Cody!" Annie yelled. "Don't touch him!"

Cody complied. Gordon abandoned the boxes of crayons altogether and hobbled down the aisle to pull a pair of scissors off the rack. *I can't let him stab himself!* Annie grabbed his arm and pulled him into the center of the aisle so all the school supplies were out of reach. Step-by-step, pulling him by the arm, she forced him to the end of the aisle. He strained and fought against her, grunting and squawking. Annie wanted to comfort him, but she was having a hard enough time concentrating on not dropping the pint of milk, box of crayons, and her journal. They reached the checkout lane. With one hand gripping his wrist, she dropped her journal, the milk and the crayons onto the conveyor belt.

Angela was staring with her mouth open. "Annie, honey, what in the hell is going on?"

Annie held her chin high in the air. She acted as though she was too focused on trying to get Cody's attention and hadn't heard Angela's question. In truth, she just didn't know what to say. *Can't you see I don't know what's going on? Can't you see I'm just trying not to let him injure himself or run up a bill my family will never be able to pay?* she wanted to yell.

In the narrow checkout lane, Gordon was able to reach the display shelves on both sides. He pulled a magazine off the rack. *Holding him by the arm isn't going to work here,* Annie realized. She wrapped her arms around him as though she were giving him a big bear hug. Gordon responded by throwing his head back to head-butt her and squawking like an angry bird. Annie leaned her head back and to the side, out of his range. She knew she was upsetting him by restraining his arms, but she didn't know what else to do. *I'm not hurting him. I'm keeping him from hurting himself,* she tried to convince herself. *Think about how he grabbed those scissors!*

Over his squawks, she ordered Cody, "Get a pad of white construction paper for me!"

Cody stared at her with the same blank expression she was now used to receiving from Gordon.

"Cody, please!" she pleaded. *Will no one help me?* Blinking her eyes as though he'd just woken up, Cody retreated to the cereal aisle. Annie focused her attention back to Gordon. *I've got to calm him down!* She could see that his ears and the back of his neck were bright red from his straining. "Shhh, calm down, buddy. Shhh. Let me tell you what we're going to do. We're going to pay for your milk, crayons and paper.

Then we're going to walk home together. But you need to calm down. Shhh."

By the time Cody returned with the paper, the frequency of Gordon's squawking and head-butting slowed enough for Annie to reach into her pocket for the money she owed. Angela still stared at her, or rather at Gordon, with her mouth open. *One would think she's never seen someone disabled*, Annie thought before saying, "Please Angela, can you put the items into a plastic bag for me to carry home?" *And close your mouth while you're at it.* Angela nodded but otherwise didn't move. Annie heard Cody snort as he squeezed past her and Gordon and move to the plastic bags. He packed the milk, crayons, and paper into a bag and then placed the bag into another bag to reinforce it for their walk home. Angela handed Annie her change. Annie crumpled the bills around the coins and smashed them deep into her pocket.

Cody held out the bag for Annie to slide her fingers through. As she did, she saw he'd packed her journal between the crayons and paper pad. During the excitement with Gordon, she'd forgotten he'd read her journal.

"Do you need any help home?" Cody asked.

"Not from you," she replied, feeling vulnerable again.

Annie no longer feared Gordon would hurt her. Standing with her arms wrapped around him, she realized how weak he had become. *Even with his adrenaline pumping, I'm still much stronger. Another sign he's ill.* She tested Gordon by loosening her arms. He stood still. She took Gordon's hand. "Let's go," she said, leading him outside. As she helped him walk through the automatic doors, she heard Angela ask Cody what in the world was going on. The door closed before Annie could hear his response.

The walk home was surprisingly pleasant. Gordon must have tired himself out straining against Annie. He obediently walked beside her, giving Annie a chance to catch her breath and make a real plan for the evening. Glancing at her wrist watch, she discovered it was after five. *I'm going to set him up at the kitchen table with his artwork while I make dinner. Then I'm going to put his pajamas on him and send him to bed. He went to sleep early last night. With all he's gone through today, hopefully he'll be tired early tonight, too.*

But Gordon had different plans, starting with his decision to not enter the apartment. Their walk home had been pleasant with the two of them walking hand in hand. Annie hadn't expected this new fight. She wasn't positioned to be able to wrap her arms around him again. As he turned to run down the driveway she grabbed hold of his wrist with her free hand, her other hand grasping the inner doorframe. From the odd position of being spread-eagle, she fought to pull him into the living room.

"I'm prepared to hold you here until you give up," she said above his squawking.

After what seemed like forever, long enough for two cars and one truck to pass by, Gordon weakened enough for Annie to pull him into the apartment. Once inside, Annie locked the deadbolt, making it impossible for Gordon to exit through the door without the key. With the door locked, she didn't feel the need to continue holding his arm. She left him jumping and squawking in the living room. She walked into the kitchen with the grocery bag. She set the pint of milk in the refrigerator, unwrapped the construction paper pad and opened the box of crayons. She cleared off a space on the kitchen table for him to work.

"Come on, Gordon. Come over here and color," she called to him.

Gordon stayed where he was, jumping but not squawking. Annie shrugged and began boiling a pot of water to cook spaghetti noodles. In a skillet, she browned a pound of hamburger meat. Gordon calmed down, but he didn't sit at the kitchen table to work. Instead, he tiptoed throughout the apartment. As he entered each room he squawked, as though what he saw displeased him. While she cooked, Annie talked to him. "Sit down here and draw." She turned off the heat, drained the noodles, and poured them back into the pot. "Relax." She drained the cooked hamburger and added it and a small can of spaghetti sauce to the noodles. "This is your home now."

Before putting his plate of food on the table, Annie cut his spaghetti so he could eat it with a spoon. As she filled her own plate with food, she realized Gordon had stopped squawking. The apartment was quiet. He wasn't in the living room. He wasn't standing in the hallway. Annie set the plates on the table and wiped her hands on a dishtowel. "Gordon, where are you?" she called. She found him in the bathroom, kneeling in front of the toilet, trying to lick the water in the toilet bowl.

"Gordon!" she yelled. She stared at him in shock, not sure what to do. *If I pull him away, he'll fight me.* She ran to the kitchen. *He's licking the water. I'll offer him a drink from a glass.* She grabbed a plastic cup out of the cabinet and filled it with tap water. *I'll have him come to good water instead of pulling him away from the bad water.*

Returning to the bathroom, she said, "Here, Gordon, here's a cup of water." She had to say it twice and tap his shoulder before he showed any interest in the water she presented. She held the cup far enough away he had to stand to reach it. She made him take another step to the door before she let him take the cup. He held the cup with both hands and drank. Water ran down his chin. Annie slipped behind him and closed the toilet bowl lid. *I did it,* she thought, congratulating herself. She waited for him to finish, but before the cup was empty, he threw it at her, hitting her in the stomach. Water spilled out on her shirttail and shorts. Annie screamed in surprise.

Gordon chanted "yup…yup…yup" and looked around the bathroom with a blank stare. Annie picked the cup up off the floor. *Breathe*, she instructed herself. *Don't explode. Remember he's disabled.* She extended her hand, and Gordon took it. She led him into the kitchen. She clenched her teeth to keep herself from saying her angry thoughts. *He's disabled, but he's not that retarded! He opened the display doors at the store to get the milk!* She jerked his arm to move him to the kitchen chair she wanted him to sit in. *Maybe he'll get the message I'm upset with him.* But he responded with his blank stare.

Shaking her head, she filled his cup with the milk they'd bought. She only filled the cup half full, but he didn't seem to mind. She sat across from him and tried to wring out the water from her shirt. However, the wringing just left Annie with a damp, wrinkled shirt. Again, she shook her head and clenched her teeth. *It's too risky to leave him alone to change into a dry shirt. I don't see how he deals with the spit in the shirt. My wet shirt is driving me crazy!*

As he'd done the night before, he ate by pushing the food around his plate until he was able to scoop up spaghetti noodles into his spoon. Annie had yet to pick up her fork to take a bite of her own food. She stared at him. She didn't care if it was rude. *Staring is less of a sin than throwing a cup of water at someone.* Gordon gave no indication she (or the sauce and noodles stuck to his chin and shirt) bothered him. The air filled with the sounds of their eating and drinking.

Annie wanted to be finished and ready to respond to whatever stunt Gordon pulled next. When he finished eating and was ready to part with his empty plate, she put it on top of hers and carried them, and Gordon's empty cup, to the kitchen sink. Standing in front of the sink, she watched Gordon reach across the table and grab her cup of ice. The ice cubes crashed onto his upper lip as he tried to drink. He threw the cup on the floor, the ice cubes spilling out onto the carpet. All the while his expression was blank, as though he tossed the cup out of boredom.

Annie left the ice cubes and cup on the floor. She wasn't going to let herself get upset again tonight.

"Come on," she said, reaching out her hand. "Let's change your diaper so you can go to bed." *Never mind that it's not even seven o'clock.*

“Yup…yup…yup,” Gordon chanted, taking her hand in his.

“Yeah, yup…yup…yup,” Annie said without emotion. Together, they walked into her room for a clean pair of pajamas and then into the bathroom. Gordon stood in front of the toilet without Annie’s direction, but she was too tired to notice. However, she did notice his diaper was just as wet as it had been yesterday. *At least he wasn’t sitting on the couch this time,* Annie thought as she pulled it down and tossed it into the trashcan. Again, it landed with a thud. She fastened the new diaper, being careful not to look at his hairy butt this time. All the while, he chanted.

“Mom can brush your teeth tomorrow when she cleans you up,” Annie said, as flat as the look he gave her, despite his “happy” chant.

Annie led him to his bed. She prepared herself for another fight, but always full of surprises, he crawled into bed and allowed her to pull the covers up around him. Annie walked over to the dresser and pulled open the second drawer, obtaining a dry nightshirt and pair of shorts. Without saying a word, she closed the bedroom door. She re-entered the bathroom and slipped into her dry clothes. Then she returned to the kitchen to pick up the cup Gordon had thrown. The ice cubes had already melted. She washed the dishes and wiped down the chair Gordon had sat on, just in case the diaper had leaked and already dried.

•

Chapter Twelve

"Wake up," Mother whispered, tapping Annie's shoulder. Even without opening her eyes, Annie knew it was still night and the bedroom was dark.

"What time is it?" Annie mumbled. She rubbed her eyes until she thought she was awake enough to open them.

"A little after one. I need to talk to you. Let's go in the kitchen."

Annie didn't want to talk. She wanted to sleep. *What's so important it can't wait until morning?* her thoughts whined. Mother stood at the door, blocking the sliver of light from the hallway, waiting for Annie to rise.

"Come on!" Mother hissed.

Annie rolled off the mattress and stood up. She searched the top of Mother's dresser for a hair tie. Finding the one she had worn the previous day, she pulled her long, tangled hair out of her face. Mother, convinced Annie was now mobile, led the way. Annie stumbled down the hall after her. Once, Annie knocked against the wall, causing her framed fourth grade school picture to fall off the nail. "Ouch!" she winced, rubbing her shoulder hit by the pointed corner of the frame.

"Be careful," Mother advised in a loud whisper.

Finding the frame still intact and the glass in one piece, Annie left it on the floor and continued into the kitchen. "Why are you home so late?" Annie demanded, still upset about being woken up and sure she'd have a bruise on her shoulder in the morning.

Mother set a mug of hot chocolate down on the table. Annie flopped into the chair in front of it.

"I've been home for a while," Mother said, now talking in normal volume. "I've been sitting out here thinking."

"Thinking about what?" Annie took a sip of her hot chocolate. The liquid burnt the tip of her tongue. She sucked in a long breath of air to cool her tongue. It didn't help. She sucked in another long breath.

"About what we're going to do with Gordon," Mother replied.

"What do you mean?" Annie asked, irritated her tongue hurt and her mom was being evasive. *I want to go back to bed!*

"First, tell me what happened today with Linda," Mother requested, lighting her cigarette.

Annie took a deep breath of the smoky air. She leaned back in the chair and closed her eyes. "She called me at work because Gordon threw a cup of pop at her and ran out of the house."

"That's it?"

Annie nodded, her eyes still closed. "They were both pretty upset by the time I got home."

"I wonder what made him so upset."

"I don't think she did anything. I think it was him. He was riled the rest of the day, even when he was home alone with me." Annie started to feel cold. She thought about retrieving the maroon and gray throw blanket off the couch, but she didn't want to have to open her eyes again to find her way into the living room. Instead, she tried to wrap her hands around her mug of hot chocolate, but it was too hot to touch. She wiggled her fingers in the air to cool them off. *First my shoulder, then my tongue, and now my fingers! What's next?*

"What'd he do with you?" Mother asked.

"What didn't he do?" Annie asked, not expecting an answer. She went on to tell her mom about their trip to the store and his grabbing things off the shelves. "But what's worse," Annie continued, "is when we got home, he tried to lick the toilet water!"

"He did what?" Mother asked, shocked.

Annie repeated, "He...tried...to...drink...toilet...water. Like a dog."

"Didn't you give him anything to drink?"

Annie's eyes opened wide at the accusation. "Yes, I gave him a drink! He threw it at me! I didn't make him drink out of the toilet!"

"Keep your voice down," Mother pleaded, looking down the hall at the room where Gordon slept. "I didn't mean anything by it. I'm just surprised because he didn't do anything like that with me this morning. He was just as calm as he was yesterday."

Don't get defensive, Annie instructed herself. *You're just tired. Mom isn't accusing you of anything.* She forced herself to lean back against the chair.

"He must be trying to test you," Mother continued. "He knows me well enough to know I won't put up with shit like that." She took a final drag on her cigarette, put it out, and lit another. *Keep thinking it over,* Annie thought, grateful for the quiet. Mother said, "Yes. That must be it. He's testing you. Don't take it personal."

"I'm not. I didn't," Annie replied, yawning.

"Why didn't you call me to help you like we talked about last night?"

Annie's laughter was sarcastic. "What would I say? 'Come home. He put a pint of milk in his mouth?' Or 'Come home. He's drinking out of the toilet?' It wasn't anything I couldn't handle."

Mother smiled. "You did a great job."

"Thanks." Annie closed her eyes again. "Can I go back to bed now?"

"No, there's more we need to talk about."

"Like what?" Annie asked, resituating herself to find a more comfortable position in the chair. *If I'm going to be here for a while, maybe I should go ahead and get that blanket.*

"I called the state today," Mother began.

"Have they found a new place?" Annie interrupted.

A heavy silence filled the room. "Not exactly." Something in her voice caused Annie to become suspicious. She opened her eyes and placed her hands around her mug of hot chocolate, cool enough to hold. She inspected Mother's face for clues as to what she'd say next. *Why did she wake me instead of just talking to me in the morning?*

"I was lucky enough to talk to the same guy as last time, and he remembered me!"

Annie didn't share Mother's excitement at being memorable. Instead, she peered into her mug, watching the thin wisps of steam rise from the hot chocolate.

"Anyway," Mother continued, "he said there's a home with an open bed in the city. But it's a home for adult men who have behavior issues."

"That's good, right?" Annie asked. "I mean, Gordon has behavior issues. And if he's testing me…and Linda, he's likely to test the new staff, too. But if he's in a home for behavior issues, then the staff will already know how to cope with it."

"Not exactly," Mother replied. "These men have serious problems like hitting each other and digging and then throwing it."

"Digging?" Annie asked, still looking into her mug.

"Digging poop out of their pants or their butt."

That is the most disgusting thing I've ever heard. Annie didn't know how Mother expected her to react so she picked up her mug and took a sip.

Mother continued, "It's a very low functioning house. I don't think Gordon would do well there. He's small, and he's sick. I don't think he could protect himself."

Annie nodded, thinking about how weak he'd been in his struggle against her at the grocery store. Mother's eyes lit up.

"So you agree that place wouldn't be good for him?"

"Yeah," Annie said. *Does she think I'd want him to go to a home where he could get hurt? I better clear that up.* "Mom, I want him to be somewhere safe." She paused. "I got frustrated today when he wouldn't listen to me and threw his cup of water at me. And I don't enjoy changing his diaper, but I don't want anything bad to happen to him."

Mother's face broke out into a big grin. She sighed and leaned back in her chair. "I'm so glad to hear you say that!"

Annie returned her mother's smile. It felt good to make her mom happy. *We're a team, and together we can do anything, even put up with Gordon for a few more days.* "So, they'll keep looking for a better place for him?" Annie asked, feeling important discussing Gordon's future. It didn't even bother her to know if Brad had been there, it would have been him Mother spoke to instead.

"Yes, the guy I talked to said it might take another week or two to find another home since we're being so picky, wanting the place to be close to us and near a hospital."

"Well, you better call Linda and start sweet-talking her so you can get a bit more out of your favor from her. She was pretty upset today!" Annie chuckled a bit at the memory of Linda storming out the front door, her hair wild and shirt soaked with diet pop. Mother didn't laugh, and she didn't raise her eyes to meet Annie's. Instead, she looked down at the cigarette burning in the ashtray.

"What?" Annie asked, clutching her mug in an attempt to hold onto the good, warm feeling she had at Linda's expense.

Mother looked like she was rehearsing what she was about to say. "Linda's not coming back. I've already talked to her."

Annie released her mug, slapped her palms down on the table, and leaned forward. "But that doesn't make sense! Yes, she was upset, but she was better by the time she left!"

"Well, I called her when I got home from work tonight. She said she and Gary had talked and decided it was too much of a strain on him to drive into town to drop her off and pick her up. Plus, she said she's not comfortable caring for Gordon. She said it's too much for her to be worried about him running out the door and being hit by a car." Mother attempted a smile. "I guess the residents at the nursing home weren't as quick in their escapes."

Annie didn't smile or accept Linda's reasoning. "Then we can leave her a key so she can lock the door!"

"I know," Mother sighed. "I know she's just using today as an excuse. But the bottom line is she doesn't want to do it anymore." She took a drag off the cigarette.

"What if we paid her?" Annie asked, excited about her idea. "We have a little money left over every month. Instead of using it to eat out or rent movies, we could give it to her."

Mother shook her head. "I don't think that little bit of money would be enough to interest her. Besides," she paused, breathing out a line of smoke. "I mentioned something like that to her, and she made it clear she wasn't hurting for cash."

"Of course she needs money! Neither she nor Gary are working right now!" Annie exclaimed.

"Honey, I can't argue her financial situation with her. She doesn't want to do this anymore!"

Annie plopped back into her chair in a huff. "Then what are we going to do?"

Mother's expression was blank.

"What?" Annie asked. Mother continued her blank stare, alarming Annie. *Think!* Annie told herself. *She needs help solving this problem!* Annie searched for another suggestion. *Yes, that's it!* Again, Annie leaned forward over the table. "What about Edna? She just retired from the store and has time to watch him. And as Grandma Jo's friend, she knew

Gordon when he was younger. So she'll know what to expect from him. And I was the one who got her the job at the store, so she owes me a favor!" Annie waited for her mom's response. Mother shook her head.

"Then what?" Annie asked, sounding cross. *She's not even making an effort to come up with suggestions, but she sure is quick to shoot down my ideas!*

Mother looked down into her empty mug. "I think it's best, considering everything that happened today, for you to watch him."

Annie rolled her eyes. "Well yeah, but what about when you and I are both working?" *Why is she having such a hard time figuring this out? Is she even thinking about what I'm saying while she sits there not talking?*

"Annie," Mother said, looking solemn. "I need you to quit your job and take care of Gordon until we find him a home."

Annie's mouth fell open in surprise. *What?* "Are you serious?" she asked. *You want me to stay at home alone all day with HIM?*

Mother nodded. They stared at each other, both of their faces expressionless. Annie's eyes stung with tears. She felt betrayed. "We need the money I make," she countered.

"I'll pick up extra shifts at the plant."

"Why don't you take care of him, and let me take extra shifts? He behaves better for you. You said yourself he's testing me. What if this is only the beginning? What if it gets worse?"

Mother looked sad but set on the solution. "First, we need health insurance. You don't get insurance through your job. Second, if I walk away from this job again, then there's no way I'll be able to get it back a third time. And finally, there's a big difference between him chewing on a pint of milk and doing something you can't handle. Annie, you're very responsible. I have no doubt you'll be able to handle what comes up."

Annie's eyes welled up with tears. *What about my car and getting to drive to parks and city cafes to write?* she wanted to ask. But she didn't feel safe to share such a personal dream. *I'm so foolish. I thought we were a team and she needed my help coming up with a solution. But she already had it all figured out. Sure, she says she needs my help now, but she doesn't need me for who I am. She just needs a person who can't say 'no.'*

Mother and Annie continued to stare at each other. Annie held her jaw firm. *I can't say 'no' to her. I just said I wanted him to be safe. She tricked me into saying that stuff so I couldn't turn her down!* A small tear slid down Annie's cheek. She didn't wipe it away. *Sure, she can say she's changing her life, too. She's going to pick up extra shifts. But that's nothing new. She always works extra shifts. My life is the only one that will change. Now I don't have my bedroom or a place to work. Will I have to give up school, too, if he's still here in the fall?*

Annie felt as though she was locked into the apartment with Gordon, and Mother held the only key. *Don't get carried away, Annie. This is only for a week, maybe two. It won't last forever. Besides, Grandma Jo took us in when we had no place to go. She would want us to take care of her son,* she reasoned. *Even if I refuse to stay home, it won't solve our problem of who'll watch him. And if Mom loses her job, we'll just have an even bigger problem on our hands. So it does have to be me to stay with him.* Her chest heaved as she took a deep breath.

"Fine," Annie said matter-of-factly, sniffing. "I'll tell them after work tomorrow to take me off the schedule until I get back to them."

A horrified look crossed Mother's face.

"What?" Annie asked.

"I'm going to need you here at home tomorrow."

"Why?" Annie whined. "You have the day off! You don't need my help."

Mother again looked into her empty mug. "I went ahead and signed up for second shift tomorrow to start making up the money we'll need."

The trapped feeling came flooding back. Annie fought to keep her head above water, but the thought, *I never had a choice,* weighed her down. When she had the strength to say it calmly, she listed her one demand. "I'll tell the manager tomorrow morning. But I want to do it in person. I don't want to do it over the phone."

"That's fine," Mother responded, fully aware Annie wasn't asking for permission and obviously relieved Annie wasn't going to fight her anymore. "I know this isn't what you want, but it'll only be for a little while, I promise. And I did try to make it work with me being the one to stay home."

Annie forced a weak smile.

"When you get back tomorrow from the store, I'll show you how to give him a bath," Mother continued.

"Can't you do it?" Annie begged.

"Yes. But I want you to know how to do it in case he gets into a mess or I end up working so many hours I don't have time."

Annie felt her head slip below the floodwater's surface. *I never realized how much freedom I had until it was taken away.* Defeated, she drank another mouthful of the warm chocolate milk. *It doesn't taste so good now.*

"You coming to bed?" Mother asked, picking up her empty mug and placing it in the sink.

"In a bit," Annie replied, thinking up an excuse. "I want to finish my drink. And I'm kind of awake now. I might watch TV."

"Not too loud," Mother said, kissing Annie on the top of the head. Then she walked to her bedroom, turning off the hall light as she passed the switch.

When Annie finished her drink, she put her empty mug in the sink as far away from Mother's mug as possible. She never planned on watching television. She wanted to sleep on the couch, where she could get some privacy. She turned off the kitchen light and walked through the small, dark living room. *Relish the feeling of being alone,* she told herself. *Your new trapped life starts in five hours.* She sat on the couch and pulled down the maroon and grey throw blanket from behind her. As she started to stretch out, she remembered Gordon had peed on the far cushion.

She bolted back up and reweighed her options, minimizing the appeal of sleeping on the couch. Wrapping herself in the blanket, Annie crept down the hall and sat outside Mother's bedroom. She leaned against the wall, across from the framed picture she'd knocked off the wall. She wanted to kick the picture to wipe off her goofy fourth grade smile, but she didn't. She could hear Gordon tossing in bed. She thought about checking on him, but then she decided Mother could be responsible for him when home. When she heard Mother's rhythmic snores, Annie crawled to her mattress to go to sleep.

Chapter Thirteen

Annie hoped she'd wake to find the trapped feeling gone. But it wasn't. She felt it as she lathered soap in her washcloth during her shower, pulled a clean t-shirt over her head while dressing, brushed her teeth, and tied her shoes. She felt it as she unlocked the door, stepped outside, relocked the deadbolt and as she began her short and final walk to work. Even though the sky was blue and the sun shining, her focus was on the trapped feeling. It was as if she had a thick barge rope tied around her ankle, anchoring her to the apartment. The rope, heavy and gritty with sand, rubbed against her ankle, becoming more painful with each step.

Angela was working the only opened checkout lane. Annie smiled hello and pulled out a folded poem from her pocket, hoping Angela would think it was a grocery list. She wanted to avoid questions about yesterday's failed outing with Gordon and about what she was doing at work so early before her shift. Annie began to unfold the paper, to continue the shopping facade. *Of course, I don't have any money on me, which will make my "shopping" look even more suspicious when I leave empty-handed. I'll have to sneak out the delivery door. It's not the most direct route home, but I'm in no hurry. I'll be spending plenty of time at home soon enough.*

Annie slipped past Angela, who stood with her arms folded across her chest and feet shoulder width apart. *Oh, she's not going to be happy when I don't pass her on my way out of the store,* Annie laughed in a half-hearted manner. *She's so nosey. It'll burn her to not even know when I leave.* Annie walked to the back of the store and knocked on the manager's office door. She heard a metal chair scoot across the tiled floor. A knot formed in her stomach. *I didn't plan what to say!* Louise opened the door, dressed less formally than Cody during his shifts. She was wearing a soft yellow sundress. Her shoes were next to the desk. Annie smiled at Louise's bare feet. The knot loosened.

"Annie, come in. I was just reading yesterday's mail." Annie followed her inside the small office. Classical music featuring flutes and piano flowed from the computer monitor.

Louise was in her thirties and married to a horticulture professor at the university in the city. She'd moved her family out of the city to be in a country setting so her boys could run in the fields and not be in danger of being "attacked with weapons or approached to buy drugs in school." Annie never mentioned country kids did drugs just like the city kids. As far as weapons went, country kids drove with firearms under the seats of their trucks. The only difference was their firearms were hunting rifles and not handguns. Even though Louise was misled, Annie thought her to be gentle and kind. Annie was relieved it was her she'd be talking to and not Cody.

"What can I do for you?" Louise asked, settling down in the chair behind the desk. She motioned for Annie to sit down.

As she sat, Annie explained she needed to take some time off to care for her sick and disabled uncle until a suitable group home bed opened up. Louise showered Annie with compliments about her generosity and kindness to help her family. Annie shook her head and did her best to tell Louise she didn't deserve such praise. Louise waved off her statements and shared how she had struggled at times to take care of her mother-in-law who had since passed. "It's difficult to care for those we love. The heart may be joyful, but the service is hard," Louise concluded. Annie noticed Louise never indicated feeling trapped. *She's a better person than me*, Annie decided. *My heart is not joyful.*

"You know," Louise said, "we're supposed to require hourly employees to quit when they want extended time off and then re-apply. It's so we can fill their positions with people wanting a permanent job, in case the employees don't come back. If I make you quit, then you'll lose your seniority when you return."

"Oh," Annie said, surprised. She hadn't anticipated the penalty of losing her seniority. She felt the barge rope tighten around her ankle.

"But," Louise continued, "I won't do that to you. You've been such a good employee. Few employees have been here longer. It doesn't seem fair to penalize you for taking care of your uncle. Besides, I believe you'll be back."

"Thank you so much!" Annie exclaimed, expecting the barge rope to loosen, yet it remained just as tight. She tried to hide her disappointment by trying to look relaxed. She spread her hands out on the ends of the chair's armrests and leaned back. "I'm so glad it was you I talked to you instead of Cody."

Louise looked puzzled. "Now, why would you say that? You're one of Cody's best workers. He's told me so."

"He has?" Annie asked, skeptical Louse was telling the truth. *I've already fallen into one trap within the last 12 hours. I don't need to fall into another one*. But looking at the puzzled expression that remained on Louise's face, Annie concluded, *Louise must be one of those people who always sees good in people, whether or not it's there.*

"He's said so…several times!" Louise insisted. "You know how much turnover we've had while you've been here. You're one of the few employees he can count on. Don't you worry, honey. He'll understand about this."

Annie felt her own version of a puzzled expression splash across her face. She placed the palms of her hands on her forehead. "Are we talking about the same person? Cody Woods?" Louise nodded. Annie held the sides of her head with her hands, "I don't think he'll understand at all! He's so mean and miserable!" *Shut up*, she commanded herself. *Shut up! Louise just did you a big favor by letting you keep your seniority. Don't offend her and make her take back the favor!*

Louise scratched her head while she considered what Annie had said. "I guess I can see where you're coming from. He's not been quite the same since his grandpa died, but I still see the boy I first met."

Annie ignored the warning she had given herself. She put her hands on her knees. "But he's been like this ever since I've worked here…for two years!"

Louise nodded, looking at the calendar on the wall. "Yes, that's about right. His grandpa passed away about two and a half years ago. I tried for the longest time to get him to talk to me about it, but he won't. He's like a vault! His grandpa raised him, you know."

No, I didn't know, Annie thought as she stood, looking at her watch. She thanked Louise and promised to come back to work as soon as she could.

After slipping out the delivery entrance undetected by Angela, Annie spent her time walking home wondering why she couldn't see the Cody Louise and Ms. Erwin saw. She didn't doubt the pain Cody felt from the death of his grandpa. She could relate to her own heartache from losing Grandma Jo and missing her laugh so much it hurt. *But why can they see something redeeming in Cody I can't? I'm supposed to be the poet. I'm supposed to be able to see things as they are, in an honest way, free from the labels people often use.*

As she approached her front door, Annie was lost in thought and almost didn't hear her name being called.

"Hey, Annie!"

Annie stopped and looked behind her, half expecting to see Angela trotting after her, demanding answers. But the street and sidewalks were empty. Annie looked at the neglected apartment building, now expecting to see her mom leaning out the door, wanting her to hurry. But the apartment door was closed and the blinds in the window were drawn.

"Annie, up here!"

Annie looked into the sky above her, half expecting to see into the heavens. But the sky was a solid blue dotted with fluffy white clouds. Then she saw Kelly's head of yellow curls protruding from the second-story window that had framed the flashlight a few nights back. *What now?* Annie wondered as she lugged her barge rope to the sidewalk below the window.

"How are you feeling?" Annie called. Now that she was closer, she could see scabs covering Kelly's face and arms.

"Bored! Have you had the chicken pox?"

"Yeah," Annie replied.

"Then come up, will you? I don't think I've ever been this bored in my life!"

Annie glanced at her watch. *I know Mom wants to show me how to give Gordon a bath, but there's plenty of time before she needs to be at work. And surely a bath won't take a long time. Gordon's not that big of a man. There's not much to wash. Plus he's used to being dirty, seeing how he spends the majority of his day slobbering on himself. This is my last morning of freedom. If I can't spend it at the dock, then I might as well spend it seeing what the inside of the Foster house looks like.*

Annie approached the front door, not sure if she should let herself into the house, ring the doorbell, or just wait for Kelly to come get her. She eliminated the option of letting herself in. *It's not like I'd know where to go once inside.* She chose the option of waiting for Kelly to come get her. But by the time Annie had counted to 30 and had yet to hear sounds of someone inside the house rushing to the door, she chose to ring the doorbell.

An elderly woman, short in stature with gray hair with a tight curly perm, a woman who wasn't Kelly's mother, answered the door. "Yes?"

"Hi," Annie said, not sure what else to say. *Do I tell her Kelly invited me over by yelling out her window? Isn't Kelly on her way downstairs,* she wondered, peeking over the head of the tiny woman. The elderly woman noticed Annie looking behind her and closed the door a little. Annie offered, "I'm a...classmate of Kelly's. I live across the street." The woman's gaze traveled past Annie and across the street to the shabby apartments Annie called home. Rather than relaxing, the woman closed the door a bit more. Annie ignored the implied judgment about her home and continued, "I was out walking and Kelly called out her window for me to visit her." *I may live in a rundown apartment, but I don't yell out of my window at people!* "I've already had the chicken pox."

"Well, step inside a minute," the woman said. Annie entered into a room that was three times the size of the living room of her apartment. The hardwood floors were covered with large orange and red oriental rugs. A couch and love seat created a sitting area in front of her. In the middle of the room, a tall, black piano stood against the wall. Bookshelves built from floor to ceiling lined the other wall. More bookcases bordered the far end of the room, and a round table with leather chairs graced the center.

From where Annie stood, she could see into the living room, with big, brown-curtained windows facing the street and the porch swing. There was an empty fireplace, a big screen television set, more couches, and more bookcases. To her right, a formal dining room featured a light brown, oval wooden table with six regal-looking chairs. A tall, commanding hutch set against the far wall housed fancy blue-flowered china and silver bowls and candlesticks. Framed pictures of painted landscapes, a field, an ocean, and a mountain, hung on the walls.

Captivated by the beautiful, rich items around her, Annie forgot why she was there and didn't notice the elderly woman had walked across the room, past the piano, to the foot of stairs. "Kelly?" she called. "Are you expecting company?"

"Yes, Grandma," Kelly responded.

The woman motioned for Annie to approach. "Just for a little while," she cautioned as Annie placed her foot on the first stair and her hand on the carved-wood banister. "Kelly still needs her rest." Annie nodded. Standing in the midst of so many bookcases filled with books, Annie felt as though she were in a library and needed to be quiet.

"In here," Kelly called from the first room to the right at the top of the stairs. Kelly sat in bed, propped up by large white pillows. Kelly's room was huge! Annie tried to look around the bedroom without moving her head so Kelly wouldn't notice her interest. The blue in the quilt matched the blue in the ribbon running through the canopy of her bed. Tiny porcelain dolls, multiple jewelry boxes, and stacks of books adorned the white desk, dresser, and chest of drawers. The wallpaper pictured a repeating pattern of ballerinas posing in different positions. Annie couldn't help staring at the design.

"I know," Kelly said, as she twisted off the top of a bottle of nail polish. "The wallpaper is hideous. It's from when I was five. I can't get Mom and Dad to change it. I think it's their way of refusing to let me grow up. They're horrible."

Annie nodded despite feeling resentful. *My mom asked me to give up my bedroom and to quit my job, and you're upset because you don't like the wallpaper?*

Kelly put the open bottle of polish on her nightstand and leaned forward to pat the end of her bed. Annie sat.

"Tell me," Kelly said, her eyes wide, "who were the woman and man outside your apartment yesterday?"

Caught off guard, Annie sputtered out, "I don't know."

"What do you mean, you don't know!" Kelly laughed. "You were holding the man's hand!"

"Oh," Annie said, trying to make her voice sound bored. "The man is my uncle…he's disabled and sick. The woman was helping us watch him while Mom and I worked." Annie looked at the ragged edges of her own nails and crossed her arms to hide her hands.

Kelly wiped the excess polish off the brush and put it back into its glass bottle. She painted a burnt red streak, matching her scabs, across her thumb. "What disability?"

"I think mental retardation and autism."

"What's he sick from?"

"He's dying from leukemia." Annie hoped the weight of her words would cause Kelly to feel bad for asking and change the subject.

Kelly looked up from her nails. All of a sudden, Annie didn't like being in Kelly's room. When they talked outside, she could leave whenever she wanted. She didn't have that luxury now. She watched Kelly put the brush back into the polish and blow on her painted thumb to dry it. Her eyebrows furrowed, indicating the beginning of another one of her serious lectures. "Annie, does your uncle know about the Lord Jesus Christ?"

Annie resituated herself on the bed to keep from falling over. She wanted to laugh. *What world do you live in?* She looked around the room. *Oh yes, you live in the world of ballerinas.* She shook her head. *He was drinking out of the toilet last night. I don't think he'll get the concept of God.* Annie forced back a smile and said, in a way she hoped Kelly could understand, "I'm not sure he can understand who…or what…God is."

"This is all a sign," Kelly said, nodding her head.

"How so?" Annie asked, letting go of her resentment and preparing for some entertainment, though she still held her arms crossed in front of her chest to hide her nails.

"Right before I got sick, my youth group talked about how knowing Jesus is the only way to Heaven. It's in the Bible, you know."

Annie nodded, although she didn't know.

Kelly continued, "Then I get sick and see you and your uncle out my window. Then you visit!" Kelly waited for Annie to react.

"I don't understand what the sign is," Annie admitted.

"It's a sign I'm supposed to witness to you so you can teach your uncle about Jesus Christ…so he can accept Him as Lord… so he can get into Heaven," Kelly explained, disappointed Annie hadn't made the simple connection herself.

Even with Kelly's explanation, Annie didn't understand. But she wanted to, forgetting about being entertained. "What if he can't understand?" she asked.

"He has to…to go to Heaven."

"But what if he can't?" Annie repeated. *He's retarded. Really retarded. He can't even talk!*

Kelly's brow was still furrowed. Annie could feel her own brow start to furrow. "Then he can't go to Heaven," Kelly replied.

Annie stood up by the foot of the bed. "Forget about my uncle for a minute. What about all the people in the world who have never heard of Jesus? What about the little babies who die? Or what about all the people who have a different religion and who are still good people and do good things?" Annie asked, beginning to feel scared.

Kelly explained such rudimentary beliefs to Annie. "Well, for the babies…they've never sinned because of their age, so they can go to Heaven. But for the others, it's our job, as believers, to teach about Jesus to those who don't know Him. It's your job to teach your uncle. Don't you see? That's why I got sick again. I had the chicken pox once before. But by getting sick again, I am able to tell you to teach your uncle about Jesus so he can go to Heaven."

Annie found Kelly's patient tone condescending, and she began to feel defensive. "What if I try to teach him and fail? Will I not go to Heaven because I failed?"

"No," Kelly replied, unsure why Annie sounded upset. "We'll still go to Heaven because we believe in Christ."

"Is that written in the Bible? That I'll go to Heaven even if I fail?"

"Oh, Annie..." Kelly began.

Annie didn't even try to suppress the irritation in her voice. "It doesn't seem fair for people in the world to not go to Heaven because they are disabled and can't learn about Jesus!"

"But it's written in the Bible! So that's how it is."

Annie questioned Kelly's determination. She always thought Kelly repeated what she'd been told and not what she believed. The distinction made Kelly's religious lectures more palatable. But the force of Kelly's words made Annie question whether a distinction existed.

How can Kelly expect Gordon to understand such a complex idea as God or Jesus dying to save us? Sure, I can tell him about Jesus. But telling him won't make him be able to understand, much less believe. How can God create Gordon with disabilities and then keep him from Heaven because of them? Granted I've not spent a lot of time thinking about God, but all this is why I would side more with those who say God doesn't exist.

"Your God doesn't sound like a very loving God," Annie replied with a glare in her eye.

"Oh, but He is," Kelly replied, smiling, not feeling the heaviness of Annie's heart. Kelly looked past Annie toward the door. Annie glanced around to find Kelly's grandmother standing in the room.

"I think Kelly needs to rest now," the small woman replied to their questioning looks.

Annie shook her head and rolled her eyes as she walked past Kelly's grandmother and out the bedroom door. Kelly called after her, "Promise me you'll talk to Gordon about the Lord Jesus Christ."

Annie didn't respond as she walked out of Kelly's bedroom, down the stairs, and out the front door. With a heart heavier than the barge rope, she walked across the street and to the door of the shabby apartment she called home.

Chapter Fourteen

Annie announced her arrival by slamming the door to the apartment. Mother entered the hallway from the bathroom, wiping her forehead with a hand towel. "Took you long enough," Mother snapped.

"Sorry! I was busy ending part of my life," Annie replied, glaring at her mom. *I don't need this from you right now.*

Mother's hair was a mess, although it was clear she had already fixed it for the day. At one time, it had probably looked quite nice. Her hand, grasping the towel, rested on her hip. She returned Annie's glare.

"What?" Annie asked, still bothered her mom was looking at her. Annie stood with her back square to the door. She envisioned herself in front of a firing squad, which angered her even more. *I need a break from my life! I don't deserve this!*

"How late did you have Gordon up last night?" Mother demanded.

"I didn't have him up late," Annie sneered.

"When did he go to bed?"

"Early, after dinner." Annie knew she wasn't providing her mom with the information she wanted.

"Damn it, Annie! Give me a time!" Mother demanded.

This is crazy! I can't be in trouble for his bed time. "He went to bed around seven. Why?" She prepared herself for the next round. But instead, Mother's stance relaxed.

"Then I don't understand," she said softly, leaning against the wall and wiping her forehead again with the towel.

"You don't understand what?"

"He's been a terror all morning!" Mother wailed, standing up straight. "I thought you must have kept him up late and he was acting out because I made him get out of bed."

So I'm not the only one Gordon's testing, huh? I guess he's not so sure you won't take his shit! Annie tried not to smile, but not hard enough. Mother saw the edges of her mouth curl up.

"Annie, this isn't funny! We have a situation on our hands!"

Annie managed to wipe the smile off her face and asked, "What's he been doing?"

"Running around the apartment naked as a jay bird! I had to hurry after him, closing all the blinds! For a while I tried following him around with a shirt, but I finally gave up."

Just as Mother finished speaking, Gordon performed his straight leg hobble from the bathroom into Annie's bedroom. Annie watched his hairy butt as he darted behind the door, out of sight. Annie clasped her hands over her mouth to stifle her laughter, but not before a snort escaped.

"This isn't funny, Annie," Mother said, wagging the towel at her. "I'm supposed to be at work in a couple of hours, and I'm not sure if I can leave him with you!"

Annie gave an exasperated sigh and rolled her eyes. *What about all that crap you said last night about me being responsible? What's changed your mind?* For a moment Annie pushed aside feeling defensive and contemplated suggesting Mother allow her to go back to work at the grocery store. *I could pretend I'm overwhelmed thinking I'm going to be alone with him,* she schemed. But she abandoned that strategy right away. If there was one thing she was sure of, it was Mother would never quit the job that gave them insurance.

"Mom, we'll be fine," Annie said, defeated. She wished she would have laughed more at Gordon when she had the chance. *Boy it felt good to laugh. There's nothing funny in my life anymore.*

Mother acted as though she hadn't heard what Annie said and continued to look confused. *I guess I shouldn't be surprised she doesn't listen to me anymore,* Annie bemoaned. She wanted to follow Gordon into her room to make sure he wasn't sitting naked on the floor. *I don't want his butt touching anything but his own bed.* She started to make her way past her mom and down the hall. As she approached, Mother said, "Annie, I'm wondering if that group home didn't drug him up before sending him to us."

The suggestion caught Annie off guard, and she forgot about Gordon's naked butt touching her stuff. "Maybe there's medicine we're supposed to be giving him that we're not. Medicine to keep him calm. Maybe we should take him to the doctor."

"No," Mother said. Annie watched Gordon hobble from her bedroom back into the bathroom. *Good. He's out of my room.* She was close enough to him she could hear his chant, "Yup… yup…yup." *At least he's happy. I don't know why Mom's so worked up about him being naked. It's not like he's creating a scene out in public, embarrassing her in front of gossipy people!* Mother interrupted Annie's thoughts. "His med book came in the mail this morning while you were gone doing whatever it was you were doing for so long." Annie opened her mouth to protest, but Mother continued. "He's not on any special medicine. In fact, he's not on any medication."

"Not even for the leukemia?" Annie asked, surprised.

"From what I can tell by reading his med book, they've not given him any medication for a long time. I guess I'm not surprised. He doesn't talk or whine or indicate he's in pain. You know, I remember when I called the home to let them know Grandma Jo died, the manager told me if Gordon wasn't disabled, he'd be dead by now."

"What does that mean?" Annie asked. Mother had a solemn look in her eyes, reminding Annie of the depression she'd suffered. Annie felt a ripple of fear wash over her. *Don't be silly, Annie. Mom's much better now. She won't slip again.* But it was habit for Annie to react strongly. It had been a difficult time for her. Even at her young age, she knew her working to support the family meant saying goodbye to a part of her childhood…the part with lazy days spent watching TV or hanging out with friends and violating curfew. But crying about it wouldn't have helped her mom's recovery.

Mother answered, "Because he's disabled, he doesn't get it that he's so sick he should be dead by now. So he keeps on living."

I didn't know he was that sick! Annie wondered if it was okay for her to laugh at the hairy butt of a man so close to death. *Sure it's okay,* she thought, sarcasm seeping in, thinking about her time at Kelly's house. *So long as I also believe in Jesus.*

"Are you sure you're going to be okay alone with him today?" Mother asked, wanting Annie to respond in the affirmative.

"Yes," Annie obeyed. "I don't care if he's naked, so long as he's happy. I only get nervous when he starts to squawk." *I'll just lock him inside the house if he wants to be naked*, she thought. *As if I would have kept the door unlocked if he were clothed?*

Mother nodded, giving her brow a final wipe with the hand towel. "Let's get his bath done so we can eat lunch together before I have to leave." Annie followed Mother to the doorway of the tiny bathroom. *All three of us won't fit in here,* Annie thought, justifying her decision to remain in the doorway. Gordon sat on the toilet leaning over his knees, touching his toes. He seemed oblivious to the fact he was no longer alone.

"You might want to go through his binder today to see if he has a toilet schedule," Mother suggested. "The binder will also have info about his medical history, diagnoses, and independent living skills goals. The technical stuff may be hard to read, but the notes the staff wrote to each other are easier to understand."

"Could he live independently?" Annie asked, thinking again about the grocery store incident. "I don't think he can. So what's the point of teaching him skills?" She rested her head against the door frame.

Mother got Gordon's attention by waving her hand in front of his face. She turned on the bathtub faucet and adjusted the dial until the water reached the right temperature. She blocked the drain with the rubber plug and added some liquid soap to the water pooling in the tub. Then she pointed to Gordon. He stood up and held onto her shoulder as he stepped over the tub's side. Annie fought the urge to look away to give him privacy. *I better make sure I don't miss something important in case I ever have to do it.*

"I think independent living skills are something every group home uses, no matter how disabled someone is," Mother said more to Gordon than to Annie.

But he's going to die. What's the point?

As Gordon stood in the tub, Mother swirled the water to dissolve the soap. "He's in that diaper all day. If you give him a bath, pour some soap into the water and let him soak for a while."

Mother didn't look over her shoulder for a response, so she didn't receive one. Annie was busy studying Gordon, purposefully not looking at his penis. After kicking the water for a while, splashing some over the edge of the tub and causing Mother to ask Annie to fetch a towel, he sat down. "Yup…yup…yup," he chanted, holding his hands under the water as it poured from the faucet. He cupped his hands so the water collected in his palms and spilled over the sides of his thumbs. Annie stepped to the far end of the tub, behind Gordon, and touched the water to see how warm it was. She found it too cold for her liking, but it didn't seem to bother Gordon, who was still fixated on the faucet. Annie returned to her place in the doorway.

Mother squirted some two-in-one shampoo and conditioner on the top of Gordon's head and worked up a lather. Gordon continued to play in the water, oblivious to the washing. When it came time to rinse his hair, Mother placed her left hand on his forehead and gently pushed his head so he was leaning back. He grasped the sides of the tub to keep his balance. With her right hand, Mother filled a plastic cup with water, a cup she had relocated to the bathroom for this very purpose, and rinsed his hair. Gordon didn't resist her. *I hope I'll be as lucky if I ever have to do this,* Annie thought. *Lucky,* she scoffed. *Lucky to wash an old man....*

Mother then worked up a lather in a washcloth with the bar of soap and picked up one of Gordon's feet. Again, he leaned back and grasped the sides of the tub to keep his balance. But he didn't mind. He observed Mother, with his blank stare, washing his feet. She took great care in washing between his toes. *I don't even do that for my own feet!* After both feet were clean, Mother sat him up and picked up his arm to wash. "What the hell is this?" she called out.

"What?" Annie asked, taking a step to the tub.

"There are bruises on his wrist!" Mother picked up Gordon's other arm. "And here, too!" Annie looked over Mother's shoulder at the row of bruises on both of Gordon's arms by his wrists. Mother continued, "Oh, honey, what did Linda do to you? No wonder you were upset yesterday...and today. You're probably afraid to see her again. Well, she's not coming. She won't hurt you anymore." Mother started to wash his forearm.

Annie staggered backward, out of the bathroom, stopping at the hall's far wall. She knew Linda hadn't caused the bruises on his wrists. She had. *I must have bruised him yesterday, trying to pull him away from the crayons at the grocery store and then into the apartment.* The feeling of pain in her stomach returned. *I know what the feeling is now. It's the feeling of being a hypocrite. I had judged Linda and accused her of neglecting Gordon. Then I treated him even worse!* Annie lowered her head into her open hands. *Linda didn't change his diaper, but neither did I.*

The final steps of Gordon's bath were lost on Annie. She had slid down the wall and sat with her head in her hands. She didn't pay attention to how Mother washed his privates or dried him off. She didn't watch Mother dressing him or shaving him, the other thing Annie wanted to see because she had never used an electric razor. Mother continued to console Gordon, who didn't seem the least bit upset, by telling him he'd never see Linda again. Annie sat in the hall, lost in her thoughts. *Who have I become these past few days? I've been so upset about having to change my life I didn't think twice about using enough force to bruise him.*

Sitting on the floor in the hall, Annie promised to change. *I'm going to become the person I want to be. I won't be upset about sharing my bedroom. I won't be upset about quitting my job. I won't pull on Gordon's arms to get him to move where I want. I won't even laugh at his hairy butt if he runs around naked. I'll read his binder and try to understand every word of it. I'll follow the independent living skills goals and help Gordon accomplish them. I'll make Grandma Jo proud of me. I'll make my mom proud of me.*

But first, Annie knew she had to tell her mom the truth about Gordon's bruises. Her opportunity came as the three of them sat down at the kitchen table to eat lunch. Annie had fixed sandwiches, using some of Linda's mustard. They ate in silence. Then Mother slammed her fist down on the table and said, "I tell you, Annie. I keep thinking about putting it off until I'm calm, but every time I think about those bruises, I get so mad I think I should go over to her house right now. I'll take Gordon with me, of course, so she can see what she's done."

Without warning, tears sprung to Annie's eyes and flowed down her cheeks. She cleared her throat. She had a hard time hearing herself over her heart's pounding. "Mom?"

"What Annie?" Mother snapped. Then seeing Annie's tears, she reached out and touched Annie's arm and said, "I'm sorry, honey. I'm upset at Linda, not you. You know that, right?"

How am I going to tell her it was me? Annie lost her nerve. She sniffed and asked, "What good will it do to say anything to her? I mean, she won't be caring for him anymore. Maybe we should just let it go."

"Let it go? What good will it do?" The anger returned to Mother's voice. "She bullied him…just like the kids at school did when we were young. They never just left him alone. I didn't stick up for him then because I cared too much about what other people thought. But I can stick up for him now, and I'm going to. Linda has to know she can't get away with this!"

Gordon ate his sandwich. Bread crumbs stuck to his chin. He had a small dot of mustard on his nose. He didn't pay any attention to either of them. A fresh set of tears streamed down Annie's cheeks, and she choked back a sob. *I feel so ashamed.* Mother calmed her voice and tried to console Annie with the same voice she had used to console Gordon in the bathroom. "Honey, stop crying. It'll be okay. I'm not going to hurt her. I'm just going to give her a piece of my mind."

Annie shook her head, sniffing again and wiping it with the back of her hand. Mother left her seat and knelt in front of Annie, her hands on Annie's knees. "Tell me, honey," she said, as if Annie were five years old instead of 15.

"It was me," Annie spurted out. "I made the bruises trying to pull him…in the grocery…away from crayons…and at home…to get him inside." She couldn't speak any more coherently. Mother retracted her hands, looked down at the floor and rocked back on her heels. She blew out a long breath of air, wishing she had a cigarette.

"I'm sorry," Annie whispered. She looked at Gordon and told him, too, in a louder voice, although he was still lost in his sandwich. Mother didn't say anything, but she returned her hands to Annie's knees and kept them there until Annie stopped crying. After Gordon finished his sandwich, he licked his fingers. He picked up his empty cup and looked into it for water. Finding none, he threw it onto the floor. Annie wiped her eyes with the back of her hand. She looked at her watch. It was time for Mother to leave for work.

"Your shift," Annie whispered.

Mother nodded, but she stayed put. Annie was afraid of what she'd say. *She doesn't know I've promised to change.*

"Thanks for not letting me storm over to Linda's."

Annie nodded, still sniffling.

"I know you didn't mean to bruise him."

Annie shook her head.

"And knowing how well you do in tough situations, I doubt I would have been able to do any better."

Annie managed a small, grateful smile.

"Are you sure you'll be okay with him today?" Mother asked, standing.

Annie nodded. "I promise. I'll take care of him."

Mother began to load her bag for work. She didn't speak. Neither did Annie, who picked up Gordon's cup off the floor. She carried it and the lunch plates to the kitchen sink. She hadn't finished her lunch, but she wasn't hungry. Gordon reached for Annie's glass of water. She didn't stop him. He drank the rest of the water in one long drink. Mother kissed Annie on the cheek and left for work. Not another word was spoken about the bruises.

Chapter Fifteen

With her nose still running enough to cause her to sniff every now and then, Annie placed Gordon's new paper pad and crayon box in front of him as he sat at the kitchen table. He began to fidget in his seat. She started to open the box of crayons, but Gordon took them from her, not wanting the help. He set them down to his side. Annie retreated into the living room to watch him. He stopped fidgeting and opened the paper pad, flipping through the blank pages before settling on one. He tore it from the pad, placed it before him on the table, and set the rest to the side. Next, he focused his attention back to the opened box of crayons. With the tips of his fingers, he picked up each one by its pointed end and re-located it in the box until they all were organized in the order he desired.

Annie took a seat on the arm of the couch, sensing she was watching an artist at work. *Crayons are the medium.* Gordon's movements were smooth as a fish navigating itself through familiar water. He leaned over his paper and, clutching a purple crayon in his right hand, began drawing a large circle in the center. *He's focused on his art. I'd like to think that's what I look like sitting at the dock, writing.* She fought the urge to approach him and kneel down to observe his face. *Does he look upon his paper with a blank expression?* she wondered.

Inspired by Gordon's creative process, Annie wished she could pick up her journal and leave him sitting at the kitchen table, entranced in his own world, to walk down to the dock to write. *No, I shouldn't even think about it. Locking him in the apartment while I go write will not make Grandma Jo proud.* Instead she left the kitchen and settled down on one of the couch cushions Gordon hadn't peed on. She pulled his thick binder onto her lap and turned to the first tabbed section, the medical section. The words on the page looked like a foreign language. Discouraged, she set the binder aside and retrieved her dictionary from her bedroom. *You have to at least try to understand this,* she told herself as she opened the dictionary to look up the first foreign word.

An hour passed before she glanced up at the clock. She'd struggled through his diagnosis, wishing she hadn't thrown away her psychology notes after her final exam last semester. *Who would have thought they would have come in handy? Besides, of course, for diagnosing Cody with every abnormality in the book…poor guy!* She found herself wishing she had paid more attention to autism and mental retardation. She recalled there hadn't been much information, but if she were sitting in class now, she'd have a list of questions. *Mother was right. I didn't understand a lot of the technical stuff. But it's clear the doctors think he's deaf!*

She tossed the binder to the side and jumped up off the couch to fill a cup with water for Gordon. *I'm giving him a plastic cup in case he throws it.* She filled the cup two thirds of the way full to lessen the chance of him spilling it as he tipped it up to his mouth. As she held the cup out to him, Gordon looked at it and began to fidget in his seat. Annie stared at the picture before him. A large, purple circle in the center of the paper drew her attention away from the three smaller circles on the perimeter outlined in brown, black, and orange. He whimpered as he picked up the crayon box. Holding the brown crayon with the tips of his fingers, he placed it in the box. He then reached for the orange crayon. Every so often, he looked at the cup of water.

"Gordon, you don't have to put your things away to take a drink," she advised, but her words fell on diagnosed deaf ears.

Gordon finished putting away his crayons and took the cup from her hand. He gulped all the water (that didn't spill on his shirt). Before returning to his art, he threw the empty cup over the table onto the floor. Annie sighed. *Why he does he do that? Maybe I'll read it in his medical book.* She walked around the table to retrieve the cup from the floor. As she did, Gordon extracted the brown crayon from the box. Annie walked into the kitchen and pretended to busy herself at the sink so she could watch Gordon work.

His face was intent on his art; he looked determined, though Annie couldn't see his eyes. Holding the base of the crayon with his thumb and index finger, he dragged the crayon in a circle on the left of the page. Bit by bit, the thin brown border became thick and solid. Even after the border was complete, he continued to color it. Annie could see the wax from the crayon build up on the paper. *There's nothing wrong with his eyes. The border is already filled. Why does he keep coloring it?* She shrugged her shoulders at her unanswered question and returned to the couch to continue her reading.

By utilizing the Life Skills section of the medical book, Annie generated a daily schedule she and Gordon began to follow. After waking, he bathed with Mother's help. Then the three of them ate a breakfast that also served as their lunch if it were late enough in the day. If they ate foods that needed to be cut, such as waffles or sausage, Annie assisted Gordon, who held his knife and fork, by using the hand-over-hand method.

The binder also contained a toilet schedule filled with staff initials, indicating the staff took him to the toilet every two hours. Annie guessed Gordon was somewhat toilet trained, but not knowing how well, she decided to keep him in diapers. Yet she followed the schedule in the binder. To discourage him from drinking toilet-water, the schedule also contained a water break after each bathroom break. Due to his emitting strings of "yups" as he colored, Annie wasn't worried about him getting bored or being unhappy.

In the beginning, Annie felt as though she were stranded in the river, clinging to her life jacket and bobbing in the waves. Obtaining Gordon's trust to let her place her hand on his to help cut his food proved difficult. Even after he grew accustomed to her assistance, he still fidgeted in his seat, causing Annie to wonder, *Does he trust me or did I just wear down his hungry spirit?* She also found it difficult to wait patiently as he insisted on putting away and organizing his crayons before every toilet break. *What's my hurry?* she once wondered. *There's nothing for me to rush to. I'm incapable of working on my poems in this apartment.*

But by the fifth day on the schedule, when Gordon's body became accustomed to sitting on the toilet and he could wear regular underwear during the day, Annie's foot touched the riverbed so she could stop bobbing and stand. Gordon still wore diapers at night and filled them to capacity, as he allowed nothing to disturb his sleep. He only wore them during the day if his stomach was upset and he'd had diarrhea. Still, though, she didn't complain as she wiped and wiped his hairy butt with toilet paper.

After cleaning up after Gordon's first bout of diarrhea in his diaper, which was a largely unsuccessful effort, she figured she might as well overcome her qualms about giving him a bath. She poured lots of soap into the water to form bubbles, thrilling a fascinated Gordon. *A super long bubble bath is a fair compromise for not washing his penis with a washcloth,* she bargained. *I am NOT going to use the hand-over-hand method to wash him there. No matter what I do, I draw the line at that!*

"You'll color and recolor your pictures. But you are satisfied with one touch of the washcloth? I don't get it," she said to him once. He didn't answer.

On the sixth day on the schedule, Annie nicked his lip while shaving him. He didn't wince or whimper. He continued to stand in front of the mirror waiting for her to finish using the old electric razor he'd brought from the group home. A bead of blood formed on his lip, alerting Annie he'd been injured. With one of her hands on his, they applied pressure to his lip with a tissue. With her other hand, she inspected the razor. One of the bits was missing on the circular blade, causing a hole large enough to catch his lip. Tears welled up in her eyes. *Even when I try my best to do what's right, I hurt him.*

"I'm sorry, Gordon. I'm so sorry," she apologized.

He didn't react. She threw the tissue into the trashcan and wiped her eyes. Feeling defeated, she took his hand. "Come on. Let's go color. I'll buy you a new razor tomorrow."

And she did. She woke, even before Mother's alarm buzzed, just as the sun had started to rise. Annie woke at the time her body had been accustomed to before she started caring for Gordon...before there was no longer any reason to rise early in the morning to head to the dock before work...before she had given up her writing. Despite rising as she had done in the past, she did not return to her old ways. Instead she followed her new schedule, the one she had created around Gordon. She sneaked into Gordon's room to retrieve her clothes for the day. She showered, dressed, and allowed her hair to dry as she walked to the store.

I want to be the one to replace the razor, she thought as she locked the door to the apartment and slipped the key in her pocket. *And I want to buy the best razor. The one that will keep me from nicking his lip again. And if the best one just happens to be the most expensive one, then I want to be able to buy it. If I leave the choice to Mom, she might settle for the cheapest model.* Annie reasoned with herself for most of the walk to the store. It kept her from feeling guilty about not having asked to take money from the cookie jar. It didn't feel the same spending money since she wasn't earning money for the household. Still, she felt this particular situation necessitated it.

I miss the outside. I miss the river. She shook her head as though she were trying to shake the thoughts from her memory. It was six days since she'd been outside, other than to walk to the apartment complex's laundry facility to wash Gordon's laundry, which she did at night after he'd gone to bed. She still didn't trust herself to know what to do if they left the apartment and he refused to follow her lead. She waited to wash his few ragged clothes until he'd fallen asleep so she could escape without detection. *Of course, with the way he stares at his artwork and is deaf, I could probably sneak out during the day while he colored.* But she never tried it.

Standing on the bridge, she paused to breathe in the fresh, cool air of morning. She leaned over the stone wall to look at the train tracks below. *It's weird to think life has gone on, that trains have charged into the town and then left while I've been tied to home.* She had the impression her world, the world as a poet and an employee and river-town citizen, had stopped so her world as a caretaker could begin. *I knew I would be giving things up to watch Gordon. But I didn't know my old world would continue without me.* She was like a stranger on the road to the grocery store.

The feeling grew stronger when she stepped through the automatic doors at the grocery store and saw a new girl working the cash register. *I wonder if she's my replacement. I wonder if she appreciates this job and the life that comes with it.* The girl was reading a book, a romance novel by the look of the half-dressed, muscular man on the cover. She glanced up at Annie and returned to her pages before Annie passed by. *No 'Good Morning' to a customer? She's about as friendly as Cody. I bet they hit it off marvelously.* Annie was relieved to know it was too early for Cody to be at work.

To Annie's dismay, the store carried five models of three different brands of electric razors. Annie studied the packages of each. *You've got to be kidding me! This store sells two brands of toilet paper, yet there are five types of razors? How am I supposed to know what features are best for my uncle? All of the models guarantee a close, safe shave! If just one of these razors had an older man with pale skin with a few wrinkles pictured on the package, then I'd go with it.* "Maybe it doesn't matter which one I get," Annie said aloud, with the realization she was doomed to nick him again.

"Francis used the model in your right hand," a voice from behind her said. Annie spun around to see Ms. Erwin standing by her cart. "Does that help?" she asked.

Annie nodded and put the model in her left hand back on the rack.

"Is that for your uncle?"

"Yes." Then, curious about the small town's pathways of information, Annie asked, "How did you know about him?"

"Louise told me. I came in to pick up a few things on the day you told her you needed time off. She was quite impressed with you." Ms. Erwin smiled a motherly smile.

At that moment Annie wished more than anything she hadn't spent part of the walk to the store resenting her role as Gordon's caretaker. She looked down at her feet, letting Ms. Erwin's words of praise slide off her and onto the floor.

"No, Ms. Erwin," Annie whispered, looking up. "I'm not someone to be impressed with. I haven't done a very good job caring for my uncle. I tried to do better, but then I cut..." she caught herself and considered trying to hide the razor behind her back. But Ms. Erwin had already seen it, so she kept the package in her hands. "I guess you could say I had another setback," she finished.

Ms. Erwin's gentle smile faded. "Annie, are you home all day by yourself with him? What disabilities does he have?"

The questions shocked Annie, and her eyes widened.

Ms. Erwin continued, "I'm beginning to worry about you. You're a child and deserve a childhood."

Feeling defensive at her family situation, Annie forced a laugh and faked a smile as she replied, "Oh, you don't need to worry. Mom's at work when he sleeps, and he's just a little slow and deaf." She maintained her false smile, which was too big. Ms. Erwin continued to look worried. Annie nodded her head, trying to get Ms. Erwin to agree with what Annie had said.

Ms. Erwin nodded, though everything else about her presence contradicted her agreement. Yet she regained her gentle smile. "I'm sure you're doing the best you can, and I'm sure your best is more than fine," she replied. After she took her purse off her shoulder and put it in the front of the cart, she changed the conversation. "Have you finished the poem you were working on the last time I saw you?"

Annie shook her head. *Wow, I'm just letting her down all over the place!* "No, I haven't done any writing since I've been home with Gordon." She tried writing at home, hoping she could focus on her work as Gordon did on his. But after hours of sitting in front of her bench poem, riddled with errors pleading for correction, and blank pages in her journal, hoping to start a new work as Gordon began a new picture, she gave up. Unlike at the dock, the wind carrying gifts of words couldn't reach her inside the house. But broadcast waves could, and Annie had begun spending her time discovering the wonder of daytime television.

"How do you feel about that?" Ms. Erwin asked, a look of concern back in her eyes.

"I haven't thought about it," she replied.

Ms. Erwin picked up a stick of deodorant off the shelf across the aisle from the razors. Annie looked away, to give her privacy. She looked back when Ms. Erwin spoke. "It was the second heart attack that killed Francis. His first one occurred three months earlier, at the beginning of summer. We were able to keep it secret from the town because it happened while we were on vacation. The doctor said Francis would have to change his life. I kidded him he'd have to stop being so upset when his students didn't listen to him, and on a serious note, I tried to get him to eat better. I don't know why, but he loved the school cafeteria's food. Anyway, I became so obsessed with caring for him I neglected myself. After a while, I was doing more harm than good in his recovery because he started to worry about me!"

Annie smiled politely. "I don't think Gordon worries that I don't write."

Now it was Ms. Erwin's turn to smile politely. "Perhaps he won't worry. But let me give you something to think about. Would you give him better care if you were happy with your life and still doing the things you love?"

Annie knew Ms. Erwin didn't expect a response, and Annie was glad because she knew she needed to get going in order to be home when Gordon woke. She excused herself by saying, "I have to go."

Ms. Erwin nodded, her eyes full of a sadness Annie had never seen before. "Don't forget to send me a copy of that poem."

"I won't." It was the only promise Annie could make that she knew she could keep.

Chapter Sixteen

With great delight, Annie slung the bathroom trash bag concealing Gordon's old, broken razor into the dumpster at the edge of the apartment's parking lot. She didn't want any reminders of yesterday's accident and was grateful the nick on his lip was small and unnoticeable. She could now pretend the importance of good hygiene had motivated her trip to the grocery store if Mother asked. But Mother didn't ask as Annie entered the bathroom and placed Gordon's new razor in the drawer, now his drawer, under the sink.

"What plans do you have for the day?" Mother asked, squeezing past Annie and picking up her toothbrush. As Mother applied a bit of toothpaste from the tube, Annie noticed the bristles on the toothbrush no longer stood straight. *She needs a new toothbrush. I should have made a list before going to the store.* They were in need of plenty, Annie observed, taking stock in the bathroom. *Mom won't remember something like a new toothbrush when she does her daily shopping.* Since Annie had started staying home with Gordon, Mother took over doing the grocery shopping, buying what one or two items they needed at the gas station when she bought her daily pack of cigarettes.

"No plans. We'll do the same as we did yesterday," Annie replied, thinking, *and the day before that and the day before that.* She stood in the doorway to make room for her mom at the sink.

"Maybe the two of you should take a walk down to the dock. It's been a while since you've been there."

"What?" Annie asked. She waited while Mother spit into the sink and rinsed out her mouth.

"Why don't you two go down to the dock? It looks like it'll be a nice day today."

"That's an odd thing to say," Annie muttered aloud without meaning to.

"What's odd about suggesting a walk?" Mother asked and began splashing her face with water from the sink. *She must have taken her shower last night when we were asleep,* Annie thought, noting Mother was only freshening up this morning. Mother lathered her face with soap, moving her head so her right ear faced Annie's direction.

Annie cleared her throat and raised her voice to be heard over the running faucet. "It's odd because I went to the store this morning to pick up a new razor up for Gordon. His other one broke," she explained. Mother scrubbed her forehead, unconcerned. "While I was there, I ran into one of my teachers who said basically the same thing…that I should go down to the dock. Isn't that weird?"

Mother didn't reply. She was busy rinsing the soap off her face. With her eyes scrunched closed to keep water from running into them, she felt around for a hand towel. Annie picked up the towel and put it into her mother's wandering hand. Mother patted her face dry. "The same message from two different sources? Sounds like the universe is trying to tell you something."

"Or maybe it's a sign?" Annie asked, thinking about Kelly's illness being a sign for Annie to teach Gordon about Jesus. Annie wondered if Kelly was feeling better. Annie was glad Kelly hadn't called out her window for a progress report as Annie walked home from the store. Annie still didn't feel good about their last talk. "Like a sign from God?" Annie rephrased.

"If you choose to look at it that way," Mother replied. She started brushing her short brown hair.

"Do you look at it that way?" Annie asked before thinking of the consequences of her question. *Oh, I wish I hadn't asked that. We don't normally talk about God in the morning. Heck, we don't talk about God ever! What if she tells me she doesn't believe in Jesus? Then I'd have to worry about both her and Gordon.*

But before Annie could retract her question by changing the subject, Mother answered as though she'd been waiting all her life for Annie to ask. Looking at Annie's reflection in the mirror, Mother said, "I used to think good things were rewards from God for living a good life and bad things were punishments for bad things I'd done. I learned to think like that from watching Grandma Jo deal with people when Gordon lived with us. Did you know some people thought Gordon was disabled because Grandma Jo had done something wrong and God was punishing her for it?"

Annie shook her head, still looking at her mom in the mirror. Annie had never heard this story. How could anyone think God was punishing her beautiful Grandma Jo?

Mother continued, "Town people would talk about us... about us not having much money...about Gordon. They looked down on us. After your dad left, I wasn't happy with my life and wondered why God didn't like me enough to make my life easy. I looked at how easy some people had it, being born into money, getting the best education, getting the best jobs, having happy marriages and big families.

You see, I had listened to the townspeople, and I couldn't tell the difference between bad things that just happen and bad things I thought God caused to happen because I was leading a bad life.

"When I was young, Grandma Jo was adamant God wasn't punishing us for being bad. She said a loving God doesn't make a person break her neck to tell her to slow down. She told me she'd learned Gordon's being disabled wasn't a punishment. 'Heck! We all have disabilities of sorts,' she said. I realized she was right. Well, at first I didn't realize it, but later, after she died, I did. Now I think bad and good things just happen, for no reason, and God is there to help us through both."

Annie was amazed Mother had put so much thought into God. *She's obviously thought more about God than I have. She also sees God differently than I do. She sees God as love, and I've only seen God as a big lightning bolt about to strike. But can so many people, who have such a good, easy life, who believe to earn God's favor you have to follow tons of strict rules, be wrong?*

Then a strange thought entered Annie's mind. She was tempted to ask more questions. *Was that what you thought when you were in your depression? That God caused Larry to leave to punish you for something?* Annie watched her mom pull her bangs off her face and secure them with a silver barrette. *You lost two husbands to divorce, a mother to death, and a house to the bank. And all the while you thought God was making those things happen so you'd live your life a different way?* Annie wondered if Mother's depression wasn't due to sadness like Annie had originally thought but rather was due to loneliness from thinking God was mad at her and had abandoned her.

Mother pushed small, gold hoops through her earlobes while looking at Annie in the mirror. *So she believes in God. I wonder what she thinks about Heaven.* Annie controlled whether their conversation continued on this topic. *I guess*

I should get it over with and ask. It's not like I want to bring this topic up again any time soon. "Do you think Gordon will go to Heaven?"

Mother frowned and turned from the mirror to face Annie. Annie could tell Mother wondered where such questions were coming from. She replied, "Yes, Gordon will go to Heaven, and Grandma Jo will be there with open arms to meet him."

Annie forced a smile to her lips and nodded. *Damn! I asked the wrong question. I should have asked whether she knew if Gordon believed in Jesus. Or maybe she thinks he does because she thinks he'll be in Heaven.* But Mother mistook the smile to mean Annie was satisfied and changed the subject. "So are you going to the dock?"

"We'll see," Annie said, knowing full well she had no intention of taking Gordon to the dock. She wouldn't even allow herself to imagine how it might be, the two of them sitting on the bench looking out over the water, feeling the breeze splash them in the face as though it were a large crested wave. But even if she tried to imagine it, she wouldn't have been able to because her vision was clouded with images of Gordon's bruises and nicked lip. *Is the warm sunlight and fresh air worth the risk of having to drag him home with my arms wrapped around him?* Annie didn't think so. But after an unexpected visit later that day, she found herself more willing to find out.

Mother left for work, her satchel flung over her shoulder and leftover chicken and powdered mashed potatoes wrapped in a brown paper bag in hand. Annie brought out Gordon's art materials she'd been storing on the empty seat of the unused kitchen chair. After Gordon commenced working, she settled down on the "pee-free" couch cushion to watch the soap opera she was following. A loud, fast knock at the door caused Annie to look its way. On the floor, in front of the door, was her mom's name badge and entrance pass for work. Without the pass, Mother would have to wait to enter the building with someone else or knock until someone inside took pity on her and opened the door. Annie scooped the badge up off the floor and fished the key out of her pocket.

"Hang on!" she called through the door. *I'll have to remind Mom to drive slowly. It's better to be late for work than being in a car accident or having to pay for a speeding ticket.* Annie turned her key in the deadbolt and swung open the door.

"Oh!" Annie said in surprise when she saw it was Linda, not Mother, standing on the top step. Gary sat behind the wheel of his truck, which was still running. He had parked so that he took up three parking spots. To be polite, Annie leaned around Linda to wave at him. *It's always better to be nice to drunks.* But her manners were lost on Gary, who paid her no attention, looking straight ahead out onto the street and resting his arms on the steering wheel.

"Hello," Linda said, holding out the pink cup she had taken home after her disastrous visit with Gordon. Annie couldn't tell if she was still upset.

"Thanks," Annie said, taking the cup. "I forgot you still had it."

"How's he doing?" Linda asked, trying to peer into the apartment. She smacked her gum as she waited for Annie's reply.

"He's fine," Annie answered, trying not to stare at Linda's open mouth. *She's chewing grape gum. I can smell it.* Annie stepped back into the apartment to allow Linda to come inside if she wanted, which she did.

"Hey there, Gordon!" Linda exclaimed, blowing a small purple bubble. "Look at you sitting there behaving yourself!"

Well, that mystery is solved. She's probably not mad because she doesn't have to sit with him anymore. And if Gordon can hear, he's doing a good job ignoring her. They watched him as he sat, intent on coloring, holding the crayon at the base and dragging it haphazardly in circles.

"We're doing okay," Annie said, breaking the silence. "Although we had a rough start, as you know." *Maybe it's too soon to talk about it,* Annie worried.

"Do I ever!" Linda exclaimed. She popped and smacked her gum. "Well I'm glad you're doing good, but I better get going. We got errands to run."

Annie nodded, hoping Linda would leave before Annie did say something offensive.

"Oh, ya have my program on!" Linda exclaimed, walking to the television set instead of the door Annie held open. "Our tube broke yesterday morning. That's one of the errands we got to run. We got to buy a new set. We would have done it yesterday, but Gary had his therapy." Annie didn't know what therapy group Gary attended. *I wonder if it's an alcohol support group.* Linda didn't elaborate. She was mesmerized by the soap opera. When the story broke for a commercial, she asked, "What's happenin'? I need to know!"

Embarrassed by her ability to answer Linda's questions, Annie waded through each plot line since the day before. Annie found herself being able to tell when Linda had finished chewing the answers and was ready to ask another question that had bubbled up in her mind. *She's just like Grandma Jo, completely hooked on a soap opera! Am I looking at my future self if I don't stop watching these shows while I care for Gordon?*

"You know," Linda offered, the words flowing out of her as fast as she thought them. "Gary has other errands to run that he doesn't need my help with. I could stay here and finish watchin' the program, and then he can come get me before goin' to buy a new TV! Will that work for the two of ya?"

"No!" Annie blurted out, surprising herself and Linda. Out of the corner of her eye, she thought she saw Gordon sit up straighter in response to the increased volume in her voice, but she couldn't be sure. Linda frowned. *Quick, Annie, think! How can you get out of this?* "Uh, we were just about to walk to the Goodwill to buy Gordon some new clothes. He needs some shirts that don't have holes in them because tomorrow we're, uh, going out." She was surprised at the ease with which she spoke the lie. She glanced at Gordon to see if he reacted to what she said about going out, but he was back to leaning over his paper. *He can't hear, remember?*

"Oh," Linda sulked, looking wistfully at the television. Annie was afraid Linda would ask where they were going. *What in the world am I going to say? I don't want to lie anymore. I'm supposed to be a better person!* But Linda didn't ask, mesmerized again by the program. And by the time the next commercial break came, there was a new twist to the never-ending saga. "Oh I didn't see that coming!" Linda exclaimed, her eyes full of delight as she left.

After Linda climbed into the passenger seat, Annie waved goodbye and shut the door. Relieved neither Gordon nor Linda had made a scene, she took a deep breath. Then she switched off the television set and went to the kitchen for the cookie jar. *I don't want to be a liar. I guess we better go shopping.* There were only coins left over from the morning's electronic razor purchase. She ventured into Gordon's bedroom and pulled open her sock drawer in the dresser. She pushed the folded socks to the side, revealing a small tin canister filled with her emergency money. *Even if our outing tomorrow is only a walk around the block, we're going to do it so I won't be a liar!* She withdrew a few dollars, returned the canister, and repositioned her socks.

So when do we do this? she wondered as she walked back to the kitchen. *I guess it makes sense to leave after his next bathroom break. He doesn't have diarrhea today. So I won't have to worry about an accident while we're out.* From the bathroom, Annie led Gordon to the door instead of back to the kitchen table. He followed as though he never intended to return to his coloring. Annie took his hand in hers as she unlocked the door. *Don't freak out, Annie. It'll be okay. Just be quick about it. Keep moving so he doesn't have time to think about how to get away.*

"We're going to go buy you a new shirt…some new clothes," she explained in vain as she opened the door.

"Yup...yup...yup," Gordon mouthed as they walked outside. Hand-in-hand they began the path to the Goodwill, which also took them past the grocery store. Gordon's sight was set straight ahead as he walked. He didn't question Annie as she led him past the black door mat that had unnerved him over a week ago. He didn't give any indication he remembered visiting the grocery store. When they reached Main Street, Annie positioned herself on the sidewalk so she was closer to the street. *Stay alert,* she reminded herself. *It's up to you to keep Gordon from running into the street and being hit, and you won't have much time to stop him once he sets his mind to do it.* But she didn't need to worry. Gordon was happy to be led and maintained a constant chant.

In the spacious Goodwill store with a bell which rang when the door opened, Annie steered them to the "adult male" shirt aisle. She dropped his hand when they reached the medium-sized t-shirts. *Hurry,* she instructed herself, flipping through the shirts until Gordon's chant became softer and she noticed he had walked a few feet away. Annie left the clothes rack to approach him, prepared to wrap her arms around him to bring him back under control. But by taking his hand, she easily led him back to the rack. *You've washed him enough times. You know how big he is. Just grab a few of the nicer ones.*

With five shirts in hand, Annie and Gordon walked to the cash register. *We don't have time to try these clothes on. We've already been away from home 40 minutes. He walks so slow! I need to get him back home. Besides, would I take him into the women's changing area or do I go into the men's changing area? And I don't need him running partially naked from the dressing room as I try to work a hanger out of a shirt! I've held up the shirts in front of him. They look okay.* From a bin near the cash register, Annie picked up several pairs of socks and two packages of men's underwear.

With their mission being somewhat accomplished, Annie gave herself permission to relax as they walked down Main

Street. She looked to her side at Gordon, who had become taller by an inch due to his standing on tiptoes. He stared ahead and walked as though he knew precisely where to go. Annie considered trying to let him lead her home, but when she slowed, he stopped walking. Annie smiled and quickened her pace.

He seems to be having a good time, she thought, wishing he'd start his chant as confirmation. *I doubt he's excited about having new clothes. He probably enjoys being outside.* Annie shifted her thoughts to where they should go tomorrow on their outing. *If a trip of this length is a success, can I assume a trip to the dock, which would be only a bit farther, would also be successful? I guess I could start with short trips and build up to a longer one. But then again, he might not want to take daily trips. He might be happier sitting in the kitchen coloring.*

They passed the grocery store's parking lot and were about to ascend the bridge over the railroad tracks when Annie heard someone call her name. She stopped. She recognized the voice. *No mistaking the voice for God's this time!* Nudging Gordon to move, she saw Cody standing by the delivery entrance door signing a delivery form for a truck driver. She started to encourage Gordon to take a step back in the direction of the store, but then she changed her mind. *I don't need to walk to Cody. He's the one who called my name. He can come to me if he wants to talk. But I'm not going to wait too long. I'm just going to wait long enough to not cause trouble for myself when I go back to work.* Cody waved the truck driver off and began to walk her way.

As he approached, he studied Gordon. "So, how's it going?" he asked upon reaching them.

"Fine," Annie snapped. She felt pleasure at detecting the surprise in his eyes at her tone. She didn't plan on elaborating her short answer. *I still haven't forgiven him for reading my journal.*

Cody cleared his throat and said, "Well, I'm gonna be staying at my dad's for a couple of weeks, to spend some time with him before leaving for college. I'd like to talk to you about something. Will you come by sometime?" He cleared his throat again and looked away as he waited for her to answer.

"Maybe," Annie replied, fighting the urge to ask him what he wanted to talk to her about. She turned around and began leading Gordon across the bridge. She didn't say goodbye to Cody because she wanted to make it clear to him she was still upset. *He might not think it was anything big, reading my journal. And I guess I don't need him to understand why I'm still upset. But my thoughts are all I have now. And he took away their privacy!*

She tried to convince herself it was okay for her to be mad at him. She couldn't be mad at anyone else for the way her life had now become, following a soap opera instead of writing quality poems. It was hard, but she was able to cross the bridge without looking around to see if Cody was still looking her way. *What in the world would he want to talk to me about?* she wondered the rest of the way home. She was unable to think of a reasonable answer. Gordon held her hand, chanting as they walked up to the apartment door. Annie fished the key out of her pocket and unlocked the door. To Annie's relief, without incident, Gordon walked inside.

Chapter Seventeen

The next day, Annie and Gordon began a new routine. Annie woke Gordon and gave him a bath. Then they ate a lunch of canned vegetable soup and crackers. After Gordon's second trip to the bathroom, Annie put a diaper on him and, instead of setting him up to color as she'd done in the days before, they walked hand in hand down to the dock. *We must look like quite a pair with him on his tiptoes. We're walking so slow I look like I'm a bride walking down the aisle. Step…pause…step…pause…step. I should hold my journal like a bouquet to complete the picture. That'd give people something to gossip about.* Annie giggled.

When they reached the dock, Annie led Gordon to the bench she'd written about in her poem. They sat together, looking out at the river's choppy water. The blue sky and white fluffy clouds present when Annie and Gordon had begun their journey began to slide behind a gray cloud, threatening rain. Annie found the breeze off the water quite cool. *I wish I'd brought my jacket.* But Gordon didn't mind, turning his head to the side to stare blankly at the playground. The cool air didn't bother the children from a local daycare, who were busy hanging from the jungle gym's monkey-bars, traveling down the slide's chute, and pumping high into the air on the rubber-seated swings.

Annie noticed one of the children, a small boy with curly red hair, wore a leg brace and ran with a straight leg hobble similar to Gordon's. She watched him with particular attention. *Is he going down the slide as part of the group or by himself? It's hard to tell.* She looked at Gordon, who was now staring straight ahead at the trees across the river on the Kentucky bank. *He's so content being by himself. I wonder if he ever tried to play with a group.*

Annie thought back to when she first started high school. Being shunned by Kelly in the hall had ended Annie's run with the popular group, any group really. *At least I didn't tire myself out trying to fit in,* Annie thought, kicking a rock with her foot. "I guess there are some experiences everyone is supposed to have," she said to Gordon as though they were deep in conversation.

The daycare teachers blew their whistles. As they waited for the children to gather around, they stared into the sky. *I guess we should head back home, too. I didn't bring an umbrella.*

"Gordon," she said, placing her hand on his thigh. "Let's start on our way home so we don't get rained on. We can come back tomorrow, if you'd like."

Gordon stood and started shifting his balance from one tiptoe to the other. Annie continued to sit where she was, her hand resting in her lap, having fallen off Gordon's thigh when he stood. *That's odd. I must have done something to make him think I was ready to leave.* Yet, as she stood, she observed Gordon. He took several steps to the right. Without thinking, Annie called out, "No, Gordon! It's this way!" Gordon stopped and stepped to the left as Annie wanted.

Annie stared into the blank expression on Gordon's face. "You can hear," she whispered in disbelief. A flicker of understanding appeared in his eyes. Then it was gone, and Gordon was back to being lost in his world. *The doctors were wrong! They have to be. He heard me tell him to turn around. And that look in his eye. He can hear. Mom was right!* They continued to face each other. Annie said, "I feel like you've chosen to share a secret with me. Thanks." He stared at her, as though he didn't know who she was. Replaying in her head the moment when Gordon's eyes changed, she took his hand in hers, and they started home.

Thus began their afternoons at the dock. Annie prepared for their adventures by carrying her school backpack loaded with jackets, her journal and pencil, Gordon's crayons and paper, four rocks to hold down the paper in the wind, and two bottles of water. They set up shop at one of the stone chessboard tables, which had a smoother surface for coloring than the weathered, wooden picnic tables. Annie noticed the lines Gordon now drew were wavy, as though he wasn't strong enough to hold the crayon steady against the breeze off the water. Once, Annie tried to show him how to hold the crayon like a pencil, closer to the tip. He gave a soft squawk to voice his displeasure. Annie returned to her poem. *You're right, Gordon. No one likes a critic.*

Little by little, Annie made progress on the poem she'd promised to give Ms. Erwin. Sitting across from Gordon, whether it was at the dock or at the kitchen table on the morning it rained, she found herself able to focus as well as when she sat alone on the steps before Gordon came to stay. Even with her progress, Gordon put her to shame with the intense focus he gave his work. In the best of times, when words flowed through Annie's pencil onto the page, she could still be distracted by the daycare group, her eyes scanning the children until she found the small redhead boy and made sure he was being included by the group.

After a couple of weeks of their new routine, Annie realized as they walked home her best attempt at her bridal shuffle still caused her to walk ahead of Gordon. She wasn't pulling him as they held hands, even though it looked that way to those on the street passing them in their cars and trucks. She could hear Gordon's breathing was labored. As they reached the stone church, Annie steered him to the small playground between the church and its school. During the summer the playground was empty during the day, getting its use in the evenings and weekends when parents were home from work.

Sitting on a bench to rest, Annie pulled the cap off Gordon's water bottle and gave it to him. The water spilled onto his shirt as he drank. *It'll just blend in with the saliva already around his collar.* She sighed. *At least he hasn't managed to make holes in his new shirts yet. Of course, it's not from lack of trying.* Annie tried to help Gordon drink without spilling water by holding the bottle and pouring into his mouth a small amount. In response, Gordon made it clear with a soft squawk he wanted none of her help. He continued to pour more water down his chin than into his mouth. When his bottle was empty, Annie handed him hers to finish.

As they sat outside, they could hear someone practicing the piano inside the church. The music flowed through the side door propped open with a large rock. *If the door is propped open in summer, the church must not have air conditioning. I wonder if churches keep the temperature hot to maximize the effects of the fire and brimstone lectures.* Laughing at her own joke, Annie motioned to Gordon he could relax for a while. In the late afternoon sun, they played the part of an audience to the recital being given inside the stuffy church. Annie wished she knew the words to the hymns. *Not so I could sing. It's just because I know how the music of the different songs makes me feel. I wonder how accurate the accompanying words convey the feelings I have.*

After seven or eight songs, the music stopped. A frail, thin, white-haired woman exited the church. Bending over, she struggled to move the rock away from the door so it would close. As she straightened up, she smoothed the front of her dress with her diminutive hands. Taking tiny steps in clunky, blue dress shoes, she walked down the short sidewalk to the street behind the church. As she approached the playground, she noticed Annie and Gordon sitting on the bench facing her. She jumped as though she'd seen a ghost.

"Oh my," she giggled. "How long have you been here?"

"For a spell. It sounded real pretty," Annie replied.

The woman blushed. "Well, thank you for listening to my racket. I hope it wasn't too much to bear. I didn't know anyone was here. It's best I didn't, though. I'm not sure if I could have finished."

Curious, Annie asked, "How do you play for the church, then, if you're too nervous to play in front of people?"

"Oh, no," the woman laughed, fanning her face as though the thought had heated her more than the summer sun. "I don't play for the church. I couldn't! I just come here in the afternoon to play. No one is here in the afternoons."

"You play every day?" Annie asked.

The woman nodded, smiling at both her and Gordon. "Yes, dear, I do. Even when it's cold out. But I don't think it does a bit of good. Do you go to church here?"

Annie shook her head. *And it was such a pleasant conversation, my first in a long time with someone other than Mom. However, once she finds out I don't go to church anywhere…well here comes the lecture. I can tell. I've seen the beginning signs a million times from Kelly.* But Annie was wrong.

"Well, then, perhaps I'll see you around town. You have such a pretty face. I'm sure to remember it." The woman smiled. This time Annie blushed. The woman set out on her way, taking tiny steps until she was out of Annie's sight.

"We'll have to think about coming back some afternoon to listen to her play," Annie said, returning her attention to Gordon. She half expected him to have made his move to get away when she was distracted with real conversation. But he hadn't ventured out on his own. He was still sitting on the bench next to her, his breathing labored. Their water was gone. Annie put the bottles back into her bag and reached out her hand. Gordon took it, and they continued on their way.

That night after the dinner dishes were washed and drying on the dish rack and Gordon was sound asleep in bed, Annie propped open the apartment door and sat outside on the concrete step with a piece of construction paper she'd torn out of Gordon's pad. In her best handwriting, she copied her finished bench poem for Ms. Erwin. She wrote each word, being careful not to make a mistake. She didn't want to have to use two pieces of Gordon's prized paper. After copying the poem without error on her first attempt, she returned to the apartment to retrieve a stamp and spare envelope from the stack she and Mother used for paying bills. Onto the envelope, she wrote Ms. Erwin's home address, which Annie found in the phone book.

When she returned from walking down the block to the blue mailbox at the corner by the street, Mother was in the parking lot getting out of her truck.

"What are you doing out?" Mother asked, pulling her purse strap over her shoulder.

"Just mailed a letter. Gordon's in bed."

"Let me put my stuff down, and I'll come back out. You can sit with me while I smoke a cigarette."

Annie sat down on the empty parking lot and waited for her mom to return.

"Well," Mother said, lighting the cigarette in her mouth with a match, "I'm off work for a couple of days. Management said I'm working too many hours. I'm working so much that with the time-and-a-half from my overtime, I'm making more than the salaried employees!" She laughed. "So you can have the day off tomorrow. I'll watch Gordon, and you can do something else."

Annie thought for a while, not sure what to do with the gift of free time she'd been presented. "I don't have anything else to do," she said. Annie could tell by Mother's silence she didn't believe her.

"Can you do some grocery shopping? There are a lot of things we need, but I'm not sure what all to get. You were always better at that."

Annie nodded and then changed the subject. "Hey, I never did tell you I found out Gordon can hear. He turned around when I told him to go the other way!"

"Told you," Mother said, exhaling a line of smoke.

"Yeah, but I had to find out myself."

"I guess I can't blame you. My education's not much next to a doctor's."

"It's not about education. The doctors didn't get it right, and they have lots of education," Annie retorted. She leaned back on her hands, her arms straight. The parking lot's asphalt was warm from absorbing the sun's rays.

Mother took another drag on her cigarette. "When I was a child, I'd have dreams where Gordon talked to me. We'd be doing some regular thing like laundry or eating a snack, and he'd just start talking. What about, I don't remember. But I'd always say, 'Gordon! You can talk! I knew it!' And he'd grin at me like I'd finally proven myself worthy of his secret." She exhaled.

"I don't think he meant to let me in on it. I think he messed up and forgot," Annie replied. "But you're right. Knowing does make me feel like I'm important."

Just then a small blue car speckled with rust spots drove by. As it passed underneath a street light, Annie saw Cody in the driver's seat. As far as she could tell, he hadn't seen her. *He must be on his way home after closing the store.* Filled with excitement from having a day free of responsibility, she made up her mind to find out what Cody had been so eager to talk to her about. After Mother put out her cigarette, marking a dark line of ash on the grey concrete, Annie said she was going to walk to Cody's dad's house.

"It's just up the street," she said as she pointed.

"Who's Cody?" Mother asked.

"My manager at the store," Annie replied. Not wanting her mom to ask what her visit was about, Annie added, "He needs to talk about work stuff for when I return."

Mother nodded. Raising one eyebrow, she asked, "Aren't you going to get groceries tomorrow?" She stood to go inside for the night.

"Yes, in the morning," Annie said, missing Mother's point.

Chapter Eighteen

Cody's father's place appeared just as abandoned at night as it did during the day, a large, two-story dwelling set back from the street and framed with tall, foreboding trees. As Annie approached the dark house, she noticed the windows facing the front porch had been replaced with decorative boarding in need of painting. The front porch light wasn't on, and Annie considered leaving, feeling very unwelcome. But her curiosity about what Cody wanted to talk to her about was too strong. She stood in the dark and rang the doorbell.

Annie leaned over the porch railing to see if a light was on in one of the rooms at the back of the house. *Maybe everyone gathers in the kitchen.* But from where she stood, all the windows were covered with heavy material. She began to feel sorry for Cody. *If he has to live in this dark, old house, no wonder he's got such a nasty disposition. A place like this can't be considered "home" by someone with manners. My apartment, for all its blemishes, at least looks lived in and appreciated.* Then she remembered, *But he said he lives with his mother. So maybe I shouldn't forgive his manners until I see her house.*

She rang the doorbell again. *I wonder if he wants to apologize for reading my journal.* Vulnerability from the memory washed over her, and the tiny bit of pity she felt for Cody left. She rolled her eyes at the closed door. *If he wanted me to come over at a particular time, then he should have told me. I'm not going to stand outside all night waiting for him to answer the door. And I can't believe he's asleep already. He just passed by about 20 minutes ago! He's just screwing with me.* She turned around to leave. *If I hurry up, he'll never know I fell for his trick.*

She crossed the porch and reached the first step when she heard the heavy front door creak open.

"Annie?" Cody asked.

She paused, wondering if she should take off running. *No, he's seen me. I don't need to act the fool by running off.* She faced him, but didn't speak.

"I was upstairs. It took me a while to get to the door," he offered. By now, Annie's eyes had adjusted to the darkness and she could make out Cody's face. He looked at her as though he didn't know why she was there and expected her to explain.

For goodness sakes! "You said you wanted to talk. I saw you drive by on your way home from work."

"Oh yeah. Come on…" he said, stepping back to make way for her to enter the house. But before Annie could re-cross the porch, he changed his mind and blocked the door again. "Actually, the house is a mess. Can you walk around to the side door? We have a small deck area back there. Just let yourself in through the fence. It's not locked."

"Sure," Annie replied. She descended the porch steps and continued down the street and around the corner to the side of the house. The fence Annie was supposed to pass through was tall, wooden and covered with thick ivy. She had to rummage through the ivy to find the segment with the gate. *I hope I'm not running my hands through poison ivy,* she thought. It was apparent to her the side door was not used much. When she found the door handle, she had to push hard against it to get the door over a mound of built-up earth. She managed to open the gate wide enough to slide through. She left the door open and proceeded to the deck. *I want to find my way out easier than I found my way in.*

Cody was lighting citronella candles on a small round table in the center of the deck. "These are better than the porch light, and they keep the bugs away," he explained.

Annie took a seat at the small round table. *Yes, I know how citronella candles work.* She began to wonder why she had come over. As if reading her mind, Cody said, "I didn't expect you to come by." He didn't wait for her to respond. He carried the lighter back inside the house. Before Annie could speculate as to what he was doing inside, he returned with a guitar. He pulled out the chair across from her, sat down, and started tuning the guitar.

Annie watched him while he fiddled with the strings. He had taken off his dress shirt from work and was transforming back into his normal look. He was wearing one of his black t-shirts, and his hair was spiked. But he hadn't yet painted his nails or put on his eye makeup. Annie had the impression she caught him in a private transition between his two worlds. It crossed her mind he might have more than two worlds, but she shrugged the thought away.

The air filled with the chords he played, trying to tune the instrument. Annie listened to the music. She couldn't tell a difference between a string that was in tune and one that wasn't. The music from both sounded fine to her ears. She leaned back in the chair, which rocked back with her weight. She continued to rock by tapping her foot on the ground. Despite the abandoned look of the house and her general disgust for Cody, she felt quite comfortable sitting at the table. *Who would have thought?*

When Cody finished, he looked at her. "I guess I'll do this like a band aid. You know, rip it off with one good pull."

He appeared uncomfortable. Annie started to get a nervous feeling in her stomach. *I don't think he's about to apologize.*

"I read some of your poems in your journal," he said, looking down at his guitar, waiting for her to react.

"Yes?" Annie responded, practicing the blank stare she'd learned from Gordon.

"All of them." Again, he stared at his guitar, waiting for her to react.

"Yes?" Annie repeated, trying to hold the muscles in her face still.

He sneaked a peek at her, to see what she was doing. She kept her face expressionless. He strummed the guitar and said, "They were good. Like Ms. Erwin said that day in the store. Not that I thought she'd be wrong. But seeing how I had your journal, I could see what you started with and what you finished with. I liked seeing how you edited your own work."

Annie continued to hold the muscles in her face still, though his compliment caught her off guard. She cleared her throat, "Thanks."

Cody nodded, looking at her with a serious expression. "It's not just that. When I helped Ms. Erwin out to her car, she suggested I talk to you…ask you for help." Annie raised her eyebrows in surprise. She couldn't help it. She wasn't nervous anymore. Him asking her for help put her in a power position.

He continued, "See, I write songs, or the music, anyway. But I am unable to write words to go with the melody. So I was thinking, since a song is like a poem, maybe you could write words for one of my songs…a poem, for me."

You've got to be kidding me! She was speechless.

"What do you think?" he asked. He stopped playing the guitar. The air filled with the sounds of crickets praising the full moon above, a dog barking to be let inside the house next door, and chains squeaking as a biker passed by on the street outside the ivy-covered wooden fence. Annie wanted him to stop looking at her. She wanted him to continue playing. She wanted time to think.

"I'm not sure what to say," she offered. "I'm surprised." Cody looked confused.

She explained, "Not to be mean, but you act like a real jerk at work." He opened his mouth, but she held up her hand to silence him. "You're wanting me to talk to you about something personal. My poems are very personal to me. I'm hesitant to talk to you about my poems because of how mean you've been at work."

She braced herself to be asked to leave. Instead Cody began strumming the guitar and humming. Annie waited for his reaction, though she still wasn't nervous.

He nodded. "Some of the jerk stuff is because I'm the manager of a lot of people older than me. I have to be tough or they'll walk all over me. You and the girls up front don't give me much grief, but the stock guys and delivery men do. I guess I overdo it at times."

Tonight can't be real. If it's not due to the full moon, then he must have multiple personalities. Maybe that's why he has such different looks at school and work. He really is two different people!

"And not to be mean," Cody said, poking fun at the words she used earlier, "but you're not the friendliest person either. I never would have even *thought* about having this conversation with you if I weren't leaving for college in a month. I figure if tonight goes bad, at least I won't have to face you at work or school or all the people you'd tell."

"Who in the world do you think I would tell?" Annie asked, deciding to let the "not the friendliest person" comment slide. *If he can keep from being defensive, so can I.*

Cody strummed the guitar a bit more. "Well, I guess I don't know. But I figure there are two types of people in this town: people who look like me and my friends and Everyone Else. You don't wear black clothes, chains, black lipstick, black nail polish or dye your hair black. You don't do even one of those things! So you're part of Everyone Else. Plus you stood up for that Foster jerk at the store. For all I know, you could even be one of *Them*, which is a subset of Everyone Else."

But I'm not one of Them either, she wanted to protest. *And I may not dress gothic like you, but that doesn't mean I'm like all the other people in this town.* Instead, she said, "I don't think I would have made fun of you."

Cody chuckled. "Like I said, it doesn't matter. I'll be gone in a month. But you haven't told me if you're even interested in my proposal."

Annie took her time considering it. He picked the guitar strings while she thought. She said, "I've never written words for a song before. I don't know if I can." She hesitated. *Oh well, like he said, he'll be leaving in a month.* She leaned forward, resting her elbows on the table. "When I write, it's like a gift. I can't just sit down and do it. I have to wait until someone or something out there hands me the words. After I have a start, I am okay editing on my own…except for when I'm inside my apartment, I've learned. But to create something new, well, I don't have control over it. So I'm not sure if I can do it."

"I understand," Cody replied, now playing chords. "I can't just sit down and create a song. Melodies pop into my head at random."

Annie started to laugh.

"What now?"

"You really do understand. When I tried to explain it to Kelly… the Foster jerk's daughter," she explained in response to Cody's confused look, "anyway, when I tried to explain it to her, I got a lecture on religion."

Cody looked down at his guitar. He began to strum the chords louder, rougher. *What's he doing? Why does he seem upset all of a sudden?* she wanted to ask, but she didn't. She waited patiently for him to finish, just as she had learned to do for Gordon when he wanted to put away his art materials before taking a drink of water.

"Since we're being open and real, how do you stand her?"

Cody asked aggressively. "She was up at the store a few weeks ago, with scabs on her face, talking to Angie about you and your uncle. She's your friend, isn't she?"

Annie frowned. "What did she say?"

"I don't know what all they said. I figured they were saying things they wouldn't have said to your face, so I walked away."

I wish he had heard what they were saying. But I guess it's best I don't know. She leaned back.

Cody scratched his head. "Do you know why I'm so happy to leave this town?" He didn't wait for Annie to answer. "Everyone is more focused on pointing out what they think are everyone else's faults instead of focusing on their own lives." Annie wasn't sure what to say, so she kept rocking. *If I'm silent long enough, perhaps he'll start talking again.* She was right.

"Everyone is so self-righteous! Yet they consider themselves Godly people. I'm sick of the hypocrisy. People of God should be humble and kind."

Having learned Cody saw her as an Everyone Else, she felt compelled to defend the town. "Why don't you just ignore them and do what you say…focus on your own life?"

"Because they've made it personal. At Granddad's funeral, a lady from church told me to take off my eye makeup and be respectful. Another couple told me they didn't want to say anything while Granddad was alive, but they thought it was sinful for me to dress like I did at church…for his funeral."

The anger in Cody's voice was unsuccessful at masking his pain. *It's been over two years since the funeral. But he acts as though the wound was inflicted yesterday.* Annie was reminded of how her mom said people treated Grandma Jo when Gordon was born.

"The thing is, Annie," Cody continued, "Granddad loved my painted nails and makeup."

"No way," Annie interrupted, shaking her head.

"Yes way!" Cody rebuked. "He was the coolest person I ever met. He got a kick out of me stirring up this small town. He liked me as I am and never asked me to change."

"You shouldn't have to change. There's nothing illegal about how you dress." Her words of support sounded strange in her ears.

Cody got quiet. "After Granddad died, the pastor asked me to change my appearance before I come back to worship with them. It's like I can't believe or worship with them until I look like them. But Jesus was about loving everyone. He didn't set up conditions for a person to worship."

Annie listened to the notes Cody plucked on the guitar. They were low and sounded sad. She said, "I don't know what to think about God right now. Before Gordon came, I figured there was a God and I was doing okay because I wasn't hurting anyone. But then Gordon came, and I couldn't ignore all the rules I've heard from others that have to be followed for God to love you. Being an okay person isn't good enough anymore. But what really gets me is the rules apply to my uncle, who will never be able to follow them. Now I'm left wondering how I can believe in a God who would banish my uncle to Hell because he doesn't have the mental ability to believe in Him."

Tears welled up in Annie's eyes. She wiped them away. "I'm sorry. I'm not making sense."

"No, you are. You were taught to think God will be offended because Gordon isn't smart enough to believe in Him. It's just like all those different church people telling me I offend God because of how I dress. As if God is so small or petty to get caught up in fashion and overlook all the good in a person's heart."

"Exactly!" Annie exclaimed, relieved she didn't feel blasphemous sharing her thoughts. "Hey, if you can summarize all these thoughts of mine and yours into words, why can't you write the words to your song?"

"Because I've not been given that gift," he stated.

Annie nodded. She understood. "Do you already have a song written?"

Cody nodded and began to play his song. The melody was slow and pulled on Annie's heart. The beginning of the song made Annie think about fear and loss. But not the ending. Annie wasn't sure what the ending was about. She couldn't match the ending to an emotion or an experience. But she didn't want to ask Cody what it was about. She wanted to think about it and discover it on her own. Excitement about the new challenge built up within her.

"It's a very good song," she concluded.

"Thanks. It came to me after Granddad died."

Well, that's where the loss and fear part comes from.

Cody continued, "So you'll do it?"

"I'll try."

"Great!" he stood up and without further comment walked into the house.

He sure is odd. But when he didn't return, she thought, *Is that it?* She stood up. *If he doesn't come back before I count to 20, I'm leaving.* At 13, the door opened. He no longer carried the guitar. He didn't seem surprised she was standing. He held out his hand to her.

"Do you have a tape player?" he asked. Annie nodded. "Good. Here's a copy of the song." She opened her hand and received a cassette tape.

She turned to leave and began looking for the opened fence door, the melody replaying in her head.

"Wait, Annie. There's one more thing we need to talk about."

Good gracious. What's next?

"Do you want me to pay you for the poem?"

She smiled and shook her head.

"Are you sure?" He walked across the deck to stand in front of her.

"How about you owe me a favor?" she suggested. She had no idea how to value her work. This way, she had time to think about it. They shook hands on a future favor as the payment.

•••

Annie opened the apartment door and picked up Mother's truck keys lying on the kitchen table. *Good thing she's asleep.*

Annie wasn't sure what business she would have told her mom they had discussed. She pulled the door closed behind her. She unlocked the truck and slipped behind the wheel. She turned the key, without starting the engine, and popped the cassette into the tape player. Annie listened to the song five more times but still couldn't identify the meaning of the song's ending. It was foreign to her, like Ms. Erwin and Louise's perception of Cody had been for Annie, prior to that night.

Chapter Nineteen

The next morning, Annie pushed the loaded grocery cart home from the store, trying not to wake the neighborhood with the cart's squeaky tires and clinking metal frame. Keeping one hand on the handlebar, she moved her wristwatch to look at her tan line. *I probably appear healthy with this color. Now my insides match my outside. I like my life now.* She couldn't remember the last time she had felt this way. Maybe it was on one of Brad's motorboat trips a few summers ago, which until now Annie had thought of as a special time when the whole family was together. *But really, the only memory I have with the whole family is that horrible visit to Gordon's group home when I was so young.*

She moved her watch back into place and checked the time. She changed the topic of thought because she couldn't resist any longer. *I've made myself think about other things for 10 minutes now. I can go back to thinking about the song.* That night as she lay in her mother's darkened bedroom before falling asleep, and throughout the next day's morning routine, she had tried to center herself, clear her mind, and make herself available to receive the words to a new poem that would also fit the melody of Cody's song. But despite her best-disciplined attempts, she didn't receive the gift she desired.

Okay, think about something else for another 10 minutes and try again. Approaching the apartment, she looked up at Kelly's closed window. *It doesn't bother me she was gossiping about me at the store. Like Cody said, I need to just worry about my own life, and she isn't a big factor. Besides, she might not have said anything bad. Cody didn't hear what they were saying.* Annie propped the cart along the sidewalk so it wouldn't roll away and unlocked the apartment door to let herself in. Mother stood in the hallway with her back to the bathroom, holding her stomach. When she saw Annie, she rushed for the front door.

"I'll bring in the groceries and put them away," she said, grabbing the bag in Annie's hand before Annie could set it down on the kitchen table. "Will you help Gordon? He's getting sick in the bathroom."

"What's wrong with him?" Annie asked, trying to untangle her hand from the plastic handles as Mother pulled at the bag.

"He's throwing up."

"Say no more. I'll help him," Annie replied, rubbing her wrist. Mother looked green. She was famous for having sympathy flu, sympathy food poisoning, and sympathy car sickness. It wasn't until Annie lived with Grandma Jo that she got to experience someone sitting with her and holding her hair back and out of her face while she threw up into the toilet. Mother hadn't been able to sit with Annie without throwing up herself.

Annie stood in the doorway to the bathroom. Gordon sat on the toilet with his arms wrapped around his stomach, his hands holding his sides. He was leaning forward, bent over his knees. Annie noticed the trash can was in its proper place and the bathroom floor was clean. *Did he make it to the toilet before he threw up?* she wondered. She leaned her head back into the hallway to look for Mother to ask. She could see Mother outside smoking a cigarette, the remaining sacks of groceries still in the cart. *Maybe he's done throwing up.* Then Gordon coughed, drawing Annie's attention back into the bathroom. She saw him straighten up, spread his legs, and vomit in the space between them into the toilet.

"Well, that solves that mystery," Annie said to Gordon. He paid her no attention and vomited into the toilet again. Annie dampened a clean washcloth in the sink and pressed it to his forehead. She then patted the bridge of his nose and his cheeks, refolded the cloth, and laid it across the back of his neck. He leaned forward, holding his stomach, and moaned. Annie walked into the kitchen and found Mother putting a carton of milk into the refrigerator.

"I tried getting him up and ready while you were gone. I got him to the toilet, but that's as far as we got," Mother said, tossing a bag of cereal into the bottom cabinet near the refrigerator.

"How long has he been in there?" Annie asked.

"About an hour." Mother pushed the empty grocery bags into the trash can. Annie opened her mouth to tell Mother to save the plastic bags, but Mother cut her off. "We need to take him to a doctor."

Forgetting about saving bags, Annie took their doctor's card from underneath the small red magnet on the refrigerator and dialed the number. Annie heard Gordon start to cough again in the bathroom. Mother walked out the door and stood by her truck where she couldn't hear him.

Annie first explained to the receptionist that her disabled uncle, who didn't talk and had leukemia, had been throwing up for an hour in the bathroom. The receptionist handed the phone to the nurse, and Annie explained the situation again.

"How much pain is he in?" the nurse asked, sounding like she was very busy.

"I don't know. He doesn't talk," Annie repeated.

"Then how do you know he's in pain?" she demanded.

"He's doubled over, holding his stomach."

The nurse sighed. "Well, then, where around his stomach does it hurt?"

"I…don't…know," Annie replied, starting to feel frustrated. "I guess I could try to ask him to point to where he hurts, but I don't think it'll do any good…"

"Well," the nurse interrupted, "I'm not sure what good we can do here. Given all the factors of his condition, you should call 911 or go the hospital."

Annie gave a courteous, "Thank you for your help," and took pleasure in hanging up the telephone without saying, "Goodbye." She walked back to the bathroom to check on Gordon. He still sat on the toilet with his arms wrapped around his stomach, the cloth wrapped around the back of his neck. Annie knelt down in front of him and tried to look into his eyes.

"Gordon, can you tell me where exactly your stomach hurts? Can you point to it for me?" She waited for Gordon to respond, but he didn't. He closed his eyes and continued to moan.

Annie stood up and walked outside to find Mother, who had stepped away from the truck. Annie found her sitting on the retaining wall. "We should go to the hospital," Annie reported. "Should I call an ambulance?"

Mother flicked her cigarette into the grass next to the parking lot. "We don't have money to pay for an ambulance. Do you think it's that much of an emergency?"

"No. I think he can make it to the hospital."

Mother looked worried and said, "I'll get a bag of his things together, in case they keep him. That way, we don't have to make an extra trip. Can you get him ready? There's an outfit for the day already laid out in the bathroom." Annie nodded and they both walked inside.

Between bouts of Gordon throwing up, Annie dressed him. *Forget the hand-over-hand method and trying to teach him to do things by himself. We need to hurry.* As she directed his weak arms through his shirt sleeves, she wondered if they put Gordon at risk by not calling the ambulance. *What happens if we get there and they tell us he would have been fine if we had called an ambulance?* She pushed his feet into his sneakers. *You're overreacting, Annie. Just get him dressed.* She helped him stand.

"Come on, Gordon. We're going to the doctor," she explained as she flushed the toilet and grabbed three clean towels off the shelf. Holding his hand, she led him out of the bathroom, past the kitchen table, and out the door. As he stood beside the truck door, he started to cough. *Mom is never going to make it to the hospital without getting sick,* Annie thought as she opened the passenger side door and spread two of the towels across the seat. She crawled into the truck to sit in the middle seat. Gordon crawled into the truck and sat next to the door. Annie reached over him—*Don't throw up on me, please!*—to close the door and find the seat buckle. Mother opened the driver's side door and threw a small grocery bag full of clothes behind the seat.

Annie exclaimed, "His medical binder!"

Mother went back inside to retrieve it. "Thanks for remembering," she said as she sat down behind the wheel, peeking at Gordon and turning the ignition key.

"You going to be okay?" Annie asked.

"Gotta be," was Mother's discomforting response.

Gordon got sick only once on their way there. Luckily, it was after they'd entered the city and were nearing the hospital. Gordon gave forewarning by coughing and leaning as far forward as his seatbelt allowed, trying to reach the edge of the seat. With her hand protected by the third bathroom towel, Annie caught the vomit before it hit the truck's floor. Mother gagged and leaned her head out the window. *Just think,* Annie distracted herself, *a month ago, spit stains on his shirt grossed me out. Now I'm holding his vomit in my hand!* She wrapped the vomit in the towel and put the towel on the floorboard by her feet, where she could easily access it if he started coughing again.

"Should I drop you two off at the emergency room door?" Mother asked.

"No," Annie replied, looking ahead at the signs directing them to the emergency wing. "The parking lot's just across the street, and I don't think they'll listen to me without you there."

"Let me drop you off at the door. I'll park and meet you outside." Mother put the truck in park at the emergency room door and hopped out to help Gordon. Annie took the soiled towel and climbed out the driver's side door to throw it away in the trash bin by the door. She then went back to the truck to retrieve the medical binder. Mother unbuckled Gordon and helped him out of the truck. Annie helped him to the door, and they waited as Mother parked the truck in one of the few remaining open spots at the back of the lot.

When Mother reached them, she and Annie tried to take each of Gordon's arms to help him walk inside, but he didn't want their help. *Feeling sick to his stomach hasn't affected his attitude about receiving help!* Mother carried Gordon's bag of clothes and his medical binder so Annie could walk with her arms free to catch Gordon if he lost his balance. They entered the emergency room three wide, with Gordon in the middle. They stopped in front of the receptionist, a bearded man wearing blue scrubs.

"Who's the patient?" he asked, not looking up at them.

"He is," Mother answered.

"What's wrong with him?"

"He's throwing up," Annie said, relieving Mother of the duty to talk about it. "That's what brought us here, but he's also got leukemia."

Mother hoisted the binder over the ledge. "He's disabled. This is his medical history." The receptionist took the binder and flipped through a couple of pages of the medical section. He looked up at Gordon. "You're pretty sick, huh? You must be feeling down right lousy." Gordon stared at him with his blank expression.

"He doesn't talk," Mother explained. The receptionist nodded, looking through the binder once more before handing it back to her.

"Fill out this form and give it back to me. I'll mark him as a priority," the receptionist said.

The three took a seat on a bench at the side of the receptionist's desk, and Mother completed the form. Annie held Gordon's hand. He wasn't leaning forward anymore, but in the quiet of the waiting room, Annie could hear how labored his breathing was. He sounded like he needed to clear his throat. She patted his back, as if she could break up the phlegm for him. *I must not have heard his breathing in the bathroom because of the exhaust fan that comes on with the light. And it was windy in the truck with Mom's window rolled down. I hope it's okay I didn't mention breathing problems to the nurse at the doctor's office*, she worried.

In the curtained room where a nurse led them, Mother and Annie helped Gordon onto the bed and watched doctors and nurses hurry in and out. The doctors directed their questions to Mother, who looked like a bobble-head doll, nodding and shaking her head in response. It didn't take the doctors long to realize the answers to their medical questions were in the binder and not with Mother. After one more bout of vomiting, Gordon received a shot in the butt to stop the nausea. Annie whispered in his ear, warning him, "The shot might hurt at first, but it'll make you feel better when it's over." As usual, Gordon didn't react as he lay on his side for the needle. When it was over, he lay flat on his back, staring at the ceiling.

Another nurse entered the room pushing a wheelchair. Motioning to Gordon, she said, "We're going to take an x-ray of your chest." While the nurse locked the wheelchair's brakes and held it still, Mother and Annie helped Gordon off the examination table and into the chair.

"Do you want one of us to come with you?" Mother offered.

"No, I think we'll be fine," the nurse responded, leaving them alone in the makeshift curtained room. Mother sat with her head resting against the one solid wall in the room. Annie leaned forward and closed her eyes. Worries and questions filled her mind. *Why would they need to take an x-ray of his chest for the stomach flu? What if he's sick because of something we did? We've not done anything for his leukemia this whole summer. We should have taken him to the doctor when he first arrived! We shouldn't have relied on the medical binder. It might not have been updated. Plus we couldn't understand the doctor-talk.*

Annie glanced at her watch. Gordon had been gone for a long time. "He's going to need to go to the bathroom!" she exclaimed. "It's been over two hours since he's been on the toilet."

"Annie," Mother squeaked. "I think I need to wait outside. Will you be okay in here by yourself?"

Annie noticed a man on a stretcher in the hall outside their room. *He must be waiting for a room to open up.* He looked like he'd been in a fight. His face was bruised and his nose and lip were seeping blood. A nurse brought him a bedpan and walked into another curtained room. *I doubt he's going to pee into that, so he must feel like he's going to be sick.*

"How long has he been out there?" Annie asked.

"A little bit after we were brought back," Mother whispered. "I'm going to go outside and sit for a while. The fresh air will do me good."

"What if the doctors need you?"

"I'll be back before he's done with his x-rays," Mother replied.

Annie stood, wondering if she needed to help Mother walk out of the hospital. Mother shook her head and said, "Don't leave."

As though she were walking in the dark, her hands stretched out to keep her from running into things, Mother made her way out of the room. She avoided the man on the stretcher. A nurse walked by and saw Annie sitting by herself. Annie was afraid the nurse would tell her she wasn't allowed to be in the emergency section without an adult present. *I know I don't look 18. I've always looked young.* But no one seemed bothered Annie was alone. *Maybe they think Mom's in the bathroom.*

Gordon returned to the makeshift room before Mother. Upon his return, Annie suggested to the nurse it was time for Gordon's bathroom break and offered to take him to the toilet. In response, the nurse ordered a catheter for Gordon's penis. This nurse took over caring for Gordon. She was an elderly woman with rough, thick skin. Noting Annie's amazement at the thought of a tube being inserted into Gordon's urinary tract, she said, "They use these things on women, too."

Annie blushed and looked away. *I hope she's kidding,* Annie thought. *But I am NOT going to ask!* Annie stayed outside the curtained room to give Gordon some privacy. He didn't make a noise during the procedure. The nurse had to inform Annie when it was over. *Boy he must feel bad to not even try to squawk to scare the nurse away!*

After an IV had been inserted and Annie began to fear she and Gordon were becoming permanent fixtures in the room, Dr. Anderson, a black man with a shaved head, entered the makeshift room and sat on the moveable stool. He positioned himself so he, Annie, and Gordon formed a triangle. "Where's his guardian?"

"My mom's in the bathroom," Annie lied.

Dr. Anderson nodded. "We're going to keep him. She'll have to sign a consent form so we can treat him. He has pneumonia."

Annie's heart sank. "How?" she had asked herself, yet the doctor answered.

"That, I don't know." His voice was deep and calm. Annie

didn't feel he was blaming her, but she wanted to explain herself. *I've tried to take such good care of him.* A tear ran down her cheek.

Annie was more upset at thinking she'd failed rather than at the diagnosis. The doctor couldn't know that, however, and tried to comfort her. "He's very sick," he sympathized.

Annie nodded, looking at Gordon, who was laying flat on the hospital bed, staring at the ceiling. His breathing was still labored. He acted like he didn't know the doctor, or even Annie, were in the room with him.

The second tear fell for Gordon's diagnosis. She wiped it away with her hand. "The doctors have been telling us for years he doesn't have much time."

Dr. Anderson stood. "Then I hope he'll keep proving us wrong. But we need to admit him and keep an eye on the pneumonia." Dr. Anderson held out his hand, and Annie shook it, wishing her mother would return.

After Annie helped Gordon back into the wheelchair and the rough-skinned nurse came in to transport him to his new hospital room, Annie went outside to find Mother sitting on a bench.

"I thought you were only going to be a minute," Annie said, plopping down next to her. "They have to keep him. He's got pneumonia."

Tears welled up in Mother's eyes. "He's really sick, isn't he?"

"I think so, but the doctor wouldn't say much to me. I think he needs to talk to you. You have to sign something."

Mother nodded, standing. "Annie, I'm not sure how long I'll be able to stay with him in the hospital. I'll just cry and cry, and it'll scare him."

Annie didn't know what to say, so she followed Mother into the hospital and pointed at the elevators. *I don't know if I'm strong enough either,* Annie thought when she and Mother stood outside Gordon's room after speaking to the doctor, who believed Gordon was near the end of his life. *What if he looks or acts different now that he's dying?* But as it turned out, even though Gordon was wearing a hospital gown, he was the same old Gordon who lived in his own world, ignoring Mother and Annie.

Mother and Annie spent the remainder of their time at the hospital watching the television mounted on the wall near the ceiling. One at a time, Annie and then Mother walked down to the cafeteria to eat. Gordon divided his time between sleeping and staring at the ceiling. Mother and Annie answered the nurses' questions, but talked to each other very little outside of deciding whether to leave or stay the night. The nurse, overhearing them from the hall, advised they both go home and get some sleep. They stayed through dinner because Annie feared Gordon needed help cutting his food. But he didn't need any help, having a dinner of soup and gelatin cubes. They waited until Gordon fell asleep to leave.

Neither Mother nor Annie spoke during the hour-long truck ride home. The summer sun had already set. After Mother pulled the truck into the driveway, they continued to sit in silence. The two remaining towels lay crumpled on the floorboard at Annie's feet.

"So, what's the plan?" Annie asked.

"That's what I've been thinking about," Mother said. "What are your thoughts?"

Annie knew this time Mother did need her input.

"I want to spend the day with him tomorrow," Annie said.

Mother nodded. "I need to get the funeral arrangements made, just in case the doctor is right this time. I know they've been wrong before, but Gordon doesn't look good at all."

A lump formed in Annie's throat. Mother continued. "I'll take you to the hospital in the morning. Then I'll make the arrangements and meet you back there." Annie nodded. She couldn't have spoken if she tried. The lump in her throat blocked her words.

After entering the apartment, Mother called Brad to give him the news. Annie stood in Gordon's room and looked at his empty bed. Then she pulled a clean pair of her pajamas from the dresser drawer. As much as Annie didn't want to listen to Mother or believe the doctor, she knew they were right. Gordon was too weak. She could tell by listening to his breathing. She could tell by his pale skin. She could tell by the way he hadn't refused the nurse's help throughout the day.

Chapter Twenty

The next morning, Annie was better able to observe her surroundings at the hospital. The floor housing Gordon also housed other terminally ill patients, and the floor was quiet, too quiet, in Annie's opinion. *What are they trying to do? Give them time to ponder their impending death? There should be poetry, laughter, family, and friends! There should be music and colors, not stark white walls and beeping machines!* Annie walked the halls alone; Mother only stopped in the parking lot long enough for Annie to hop out of the truck with the bag of goodies she'd brought for Gordon. Mother would return after making the funeral arrangements. Annie had learned during Grandma Jo's passing that Mother couldn't watch her loved ones confined to the hospital by IV cords, blood oxygen clips, and blood pressure cuffs. Mother wasn't strong in that way.

The door to Gordon's room was cracked open when Annie arrived. She knocked, suspecting Gordon would still be asleep, but wanting to announce her visit in case he wasn't. *Did he remember he wasn't at home before opening his eyes?* After allowing time for the response to her knock she knew would never come, she pushed the door open and entered. The blinds on the window pushed the sunlight up to the ceiling, lighting the room. Gordon's bed was inclined, and he was awake, leaning back, staring blankly at the ceiling.

"What are you doing awake already?" she asked with forced enthusiasm. The sound of her voice exaggerated the room's silence. Startled, feeling as though she should apologize for disturbing the silence, even though she thought a disturbance was called for, she sat in one of the chairs she and Mother had drawn close to the bed the night before. She set the bag of goodies on the floor. Gordon turned his head to look at her. She longed to see the spark in his eyes she'd seen when she learned he could hear. But it wasn't there.

"How do you feel?" she whispered. He turned his head and continued looking at the ceiling.

The door opened and a nurse wearing a nametag with Lucy printed on it, a young girl who looked no older than Annie, walked into the room. Having heard Annie's question, she answered in a sweet, southern voice, "I don't know for sure how he feels, but I'm guessing ornery! He pulled out his catheter this morning after I woke him to take his vitals. I tried to stop him, but he fought me right through the pain he must have felt from yankin' the thing out. Then he wouldn't let me put a protective undergarment on him! I told him I wasn't cleaning up any accidents." She held her hand to her mouth as though telling a secret to Annie. "But I didn't mean it. I'll clean it up if he makes a mess."

There won't be a mess. He's on a schedule, Annie thought, smiling. *He must be feeling better than he did yesterday. He still looks pale and weak, but he's strong enough to test someone new…like he did me a couple of months ago.* She leaned forward and unzipped her backpack to retrieve Gordon's art supplies. She placed the paper pad and crayons on the tray table next to his empty breakfast containers. *Looks like another meal of liquids and gelatin,* she thought, noting the empty juice boxes and bowl.

The crayons captured Gordon's attention away from the ceiling. Lucy walked around to the tray table. "Let me take these out of your way," she said, frowning. She gathered the empty dishes and carried them out of the room, but not before apologizing, "I'm sorry about this mess. These should have been picked up by now." *Who cares if there are empty dishes lying around? There are so many more important things to worry about. So many better things to think about,* Annie thought, maneuvering the tray table so the tray stopped over Gordon's lap.

"Like coloring," she said aloud. She looked at her watch. "Want to draw for the next 40 minutes? Then we'll go to the bathroom."

As Annie finished talking, Lucy walked back into the room shaking her head. *Is she still upset about those dirty dishes or is she put out because he listens to me but not her?* Annie wondered, hoping it was the second. It made her feel good that Gordon behaved around her. *What I had to go through to get you to behave can be our little secret…right, Gordon?* Lucy checked the content level of the IV bag and retrieved a printout from one of the beeping machines. Gordon waited for her to leave, keeping his eyes on the crayon box.

When he and Annie were alone in the room again, Gordon opened the paper pad and flipped through the blank pages until he found the right one. The effort he had to exert to maneuver his arms into a position to tear out the page tired him so much he paused to lean back in the bed to rest. While he did, Annie stood and leaned over him to tear out the paper for him. *Oh, Gordon, are you really that weak?* She wondered if she could trick herself into believing his fatigue was due to a sleepless night. But she couldn't. She opened the box of crayons and held them at an angle so he could see the colored tips to pick one. He chose the color black.

"Kind of a dismal color, isn't it?" Annie asked. She looked into the box of crayons and brought forth the fiery red crayon. She held it out to him. "Wouldn't you rather use this crayon? It'll give your picture a little pizzazz." He pushed away her hand, resisting her help. *I must be going crazy,* Annie thought. *I wish he would squawk at me!*

Annie sat down in one of the side chairs and watched him work. Holding the crayon at its base, he began to draw the familiar outline of the large circle in the center of the page. His hand shook as he dragged the crayon. Gordon's paper filled with thin, wavy lines, reminding Annie of the lines she'd seen him draw at the dock. She buried her face in her hands. *How stupid can I be?* she thought. *I thought his lines were wavy because of the wind! And here I've been wondering how he became so sick without me knowing it. I'm such an idiot! No wonder he started walking slower, needing to take a break at the church, and going to bed even earlier.*

"I can be so blind," she said aloud to Gordon, a heavy feeling in her heart. *I can't let him see me like this.* She rose and walked into the hall, where she started to cry. Lucy was sitting behind the nurses' station down the hall. She grabbed a tissue from a box sitting on a side table next to a bouquet of fake flowers and held it out to Annie as she approached. Annie accepted it.

"What's the matter, honey?" Lucy asked as Annie wiped her eyes.

No matter how she tried, Annie couldn't suppress a high pitch whine. "I thought I was taking such good care of him. I missed all the signs he was starting to get sick!" A fresh set of tears rolled down her cheeks.

"Come here, away from the door," Lucy coached as she led Annie away from Gordon's room. Annie followed her down the hall.

"Honey," Lucy said, "he's sick. There ain't nothing you could have done to prevent it."

Annie shook her head. "I could have kept him home and inside instead of outside in the cool breeze off the river!"

Lucy smiled the patient smile Annie had received from Ms. Erwin in the grocery store. "What's your name?"

"Annie," she sniffed.

"Well, Annie, take it from me. I've not been a nurse as long as many of the others here." She gestured her head down the hall at two middle-aged nurses conferring over a patient's chart. "But I've been a nurse long enough to have learned that no matter how good you care for someone, you can't keep them from dying if that's what the Lord has planned. Besides, if he hadn't been taken real good care of, then he wouldn't have defied the odds for so long." The certainty in Lucy's voice angered Annie. Plus Annie didn't like thinking God was making Gordon die so a plan could be followed.

Through gritted teeth, Annie replied, "Taken good care of? He was abused, maybe for years, at his group home before coming to live with us." She'd expected Lucy to react with like anger, but Lucy didn't.

"You can choose to look at it however you want. But good can come from bad. Is the abuse at the group home why he came to live with you?" Lucy didn't wait for Annie's response. "Because of the bad, he received the good care from you, someone who loves him enough to not only visit, but to also bring crayons. How many other visitors do you see this morning?" Lucy asked.

Annie shrugged.

"Look around," Lucy said, the empty halls proving her point.

Annie wasn't prepared to surrender. She was angry, and she wanted someone to be angry at. *It's not fair! Everything bad has happened to him. He's had more than his share. He's disabled. He's sick. He's dying!* "You talked about the Lord's plan," she spit out. "I don't see how a loving God can have a plan that includes pain."

Lucy didn't respond. *Ha!* Annie thought, wadding the used tissue into her fist. *I've got her.* Annie wasn't sure if that meant she won, but she felt a sense of satisfaction.

With grace, Lucy replied, "Again, it's how you look at it. I don't see God's plan as bringing someone pain and suffering. I see God's plan as bringing someone *through* pain and suffering. I *do* think God is a loving God."

Annie began to cry again. Lucy retrieved another tissue from the side table in the hall. By the time Lucy returned and had handed over the tissue, Annie was able to ask, "How bad is he?"

Tilting her head to the side, Lucy peered into Annie's eyes, as if trying to size her up. Annie stood a bit straighter and pushed her shoulders back.

Lucy sighed. "Do you hear the sound he makes when he breathes? The raspy sound?"

Annie nodded, wiping her eyes.

"It's called the death rattle. Listening to him, I say he's got today left."

Annie nodded, trying not to start crying again. "Thanks for telling me," she whispered when she had control over her voice. Lucy touched Annie's arm in a comforting way and walked back to the nurses' station. Annie wiped her nose again before throwing the tissues into the trash container of the breakfast cart a tall skinny man pushed past her. Watching the man walk down the hall, casually entering the rooms and retrieving used breakfast containers, Annie thought about Uncle Brad. *I forgot to ask Mom what he said last night on the phone.* Annie knew better than to look forward to the next time her uncle came to town. *It'll be for the funeral,* she thought, now standing in front of Gordon's room.

She wiped her eyes with the back of her hand one final time and fanned her face, hoping her nose wouldn't be too red or her eyes too puffy. *I don't want him to know I've been crying. I want to be strong for him.* She smoothed her hair back through the ponytail holder, tucking the loose strands behind her ears. She rolled her head three times, loosening her neck. She stood on her tiptoes, stretching her calf muscles. She took a deep breath. *Now, to face the battle that needs fighting,* she thought as she stepped inside the room.

•••

"Come on, let's use the bathroom," Annie said, finding Gordon dragging the black crayon around the page in a circle. She stood by his bed, waiting, noticing how much his technique had slowed. Without prompting, Gordon brought the crayon's tip from the page and began looking for the box. Annie held the box so he could peer inside as he organized the crayons' order. After closing the box, Annie pushed away the tray table and offered her hand to help him out of bed. Her offer wasn't enough. She needed to move his legs to the side of the bed and help him stand. Instead of holding his hand to lead him, she wrapped her arm around his waist to help support his body as he walked to the bathroom in the corner of the room.

After lowering Gordon onto the toilet, Annie saw a urinal can hanging on the disability bar fastened to the wall. *Walking to the bathroom might take too much out of him. Maybe we should use the can. But how in the world am I going to explain to him to pee into it?* One by one, she discredited each possible way to explain how to use a urinal can. Gordon rested on the toilet, leaning over his knees with his head against the wall. It took a while for him to pee, but Annie found he released a lot of urine. She looked in the toilet as she helped him to stand, checking she had heard urine and not diarrhea. It was only urine, so she flushed the toilet and half escorted, half guided, him back to bed.

She hoisted him back onto the bed and swung his legs up onto the mattress. She didn't slide the tray table back into place over his lap. He was visibly weakened from his trip to the bathroom, even though Annie had borne most of his weight. She found a plastic cup with a lid and a straw on the nightstand. She picked it up and held the straw to his lips for him to take a drink. He wrapped his lips around the straw, but he couldn't muster the strength to suck up the fluid. The effort of sucking made him cough. Annie pulled off the lid and fished around in the cup with her fingers until she'd picked up an ice cube. Gordon's eyes were half closed. She held the ice cube where he could see it and then touched it to his lips. He opened his mouth, and she placed the ice cube on his tongue.

After finishing one ice cube, he opened his mouth for another one. Twice, she had to grab the bed pan to hold under his chin as he vomited the water and partially digested breakfast juices in his stomach. Once, she had to find Lucy to request another cup of ice. As the day drew on and Gordon's death rattle grew louder, Annie's desire to hear him chant "yup… yup…yup" grew stronger. Opening her mouth to talk to him destroyed the weak control over her emotions, and her eyes swelled again with tears. She willed herself to stop crying.

When she thought she had the strength to tell him, "Goodbye," she took a deep breath. Her voice seemed steady enough this time. She opened her mouth but lost her nerve. So she went into the bathroom to wet a paper towel. Gordon had begun to perspire, his body working hard to breathe. Yet when Annie pulled back the bed sheet to cool him, he began to shiver. So she tried to meet his needs by keeping him covered and cooling his face with a wet cloth.

"I'm glad I got to know you," she managed to whisper. There were many things she wanted to say, but she knew she had to talk in short sentences or she'd lose control and begin to cry. *I don't want to scare him, crying like a fool.* She took a deep breath and pressed her teeth together so that her jaw ached. Despite her efforts to focus on her jaw pain instead of her heartache, tears welled in her eyes. *I'm not going to make it without crying.* She let her tears spill down upon her cheeks.

"I'm glad I made it through your testing period." She paused and blotted his chin with the paper towel.

"I think it's funny you threw a cup at Linda." She gave a short, sad laugh. Gordon responded by parting his lips, but not in a grin. He wanted another ice cube. Annie put down the cool cloth, which wasn't so cool any more, having absorbed some of the heat from his forehead. She fished another ice cube out of the cup and placed it on his tongue.

"I don't know what's going to happen when you pass. I suspect you'll see Grandma Jo…your mom. Go to her."

She wiped her eyes. "Go to your mom. Don't be afraid."

Annie pulled a tissue from the box on the window ledge and wiped her nose. Mother appeared in the doorway. "Hey!" Annie greeted with forced excitement. Mother shuffled into the room. Annie could see tears already flowing down her cheeks. *Be strong now*, Annie thought. *You've had your time with him. Be strong so Mom can have her time*.

"Will you help me take him to the bathroom?" Annie asked, handing her mom a tissue from the box. Mother accepted the tissue, wiped her eyes, and blew her nose. She tried to smile at Gordon. Annie wasn't sure if Gordon even knew Mother had entered the room.

"Gordon," Annie whispered in his ear. "It's time to go to the bathroom again. But if you'd rather not get up, we can put a diaper on you. That might be better…a diaper…so you can rest and not have to walk." But before she'd finished stating her argument, Gordon began to struggle to sit up in bed. Annie caught Mother's eyes and gave a tired smile at his stubbornness. Mother returned a weak smile and wiped her eyes again with the crumpled tissue.

With Annie on Gordon's right and Mother on his left, they walked him into the bathroom. Annie pulled apart the back of his hospital gown so he wouldn't catch the edges as he sat down on the toilet seat. They held his arms as he sat, though they allowed him to lean forward when he wanted to. Silence filled the bathroom until his urine hit the water in the bowl.

"We should let him rest a bit before moving him back," Annie said after the flow stopped. Mother nodded, wiping more tears from her eyes with her shirt sleeve. They waited until Gordon indicated he was ready to return to bed. Again,

Annie was on his right and Mother was on his left. They walked him back to the bed. *Step…pause…step…pause.* Gordon walked his slow, tiptoed walk, leaning most of his weight on Annie. *Please don't let me drop him,* she pleaded.

At the foot of the bed, Gordon's feet gave and he collapsed into their arms without warning. Mother and Annie reacted in just enough time to keep him from hitting the cold tile floor. Gordon wasn't bearing any of his weight, and he wasn't making any effort to pull his feet underneath his body to regain a standing position. Annie and Mother both froze, looking down at him, trying to figure out what happened. *Did he trip? Did he pass out? Had they accidently pushed him?* Annie didn't know.

"Get him onto the bed!" Mother demanded, shaking Annie from her thoughts.

Without answering, Annie tried to readjust her hold on his arm. *I'll never be able to lift him onto the bed by his arm!* She managed to slip her left shoulder under his armpit and her other arm under his leg, as though he were a baby and she was going to rock him. Mother helped by doing the same on her side. Luckily, in their one big effort to lift him up, they were able to place his head onto the pillow. His eyes were closed and his mouth open, as though he wanted another ice cube. But Annie knew he didn't. He was gone. Without speaking, they waited, standing on each side of the bed, listening to his breaths space further apart. Then he breathed no more.

Mother cried aloud and fell back into one of the chairs. The sound of her cry brought Lucy from the hall. She checked his vital signs and confirmed, "He's gone." All Annie could do was nod. Lucy left and closed the door, leaving Annie and Mother alone in the room. Mother leaned her head forward and rested it on the edge of the bed. Her shoulders heaved with her sobs. Yet the sound of her cries seemed distant. Annie was barely cognizant of them as she stared at Gordon's body.

She couldn't move. She couldn't be sad. Her mind was racing trying to understand what had happened. *The body kind of resembles him, but it's not him. This person looks like a stranger. His body is missing his spirit. It's gone. And I know when it left. It left the moment he collapsed at the foot of the bed. While we were looking down and reacting to his physical body, his spirit had gone up and out of him. Even though he had a few remaining breaths, those breaths were just the end of his physical life.*

So why am I not sad? If he's gone, then why am I not crying like Mom? I don't feel like crying at all. Only to herself would she admit, *I feel like laughing. I'm happy! I'm excited! I'm not sad because his spirit is not gone. Yes, it's gone from his body, but it's still here in this room. I feel him all around me. And not in a way that means he didn't go to Heaven. It's just that he's with God now. I can feel both him and God here.* Annie felt the excitement growing within her. She wanted to console her mother and tell her not to be sad, but to be happy Gordon had moved on. *It's beautiful. It isn't sad! Not being strong enough to suck water through a straw is sad, not this. Not his being with God.*

Annie walked around to the other side of the bed, placed her hand on Mother's back, and waited for her to finish crying. As she stood behind her mom, Annie surrendered herself to the instinctive feeling God existed. The God she felt around her made her feel loved and connected, not judged or sinful. *God exists, and God loves me.* She felt it with a certainty she'd never known before. Her thoughts and feelings were united in her heart and her brain. She didn't even care she didn't have words to describe it...or to justify it. *And so now I know what faith is.*

Chapter Twenty-One

Gordon was laid to rest in the plot beside Grandma Jo. Two days before the funeral service, Annie walked to the funeral home and spoke to the director about putting Gordon's box of crayons in the casket. The director, a large man with a thick black mustache curling up at the ends, clasped his large hands around Annie's, which held the box of crayons, and gave his sincerest assurance it would be placed in the casket at Gordon's side. Annie fought to maintain eye contact. She wanted to stare at his thick mustache and ask him questions about it. The first being, *Why in the world do you twist the ends like you're a villain in a black and white silent picture movie?*

Annie walked through the cemetery before the service, seeing the casket was closed, ready to be lowered into the ground. She doubted the director kept his word. *The funeral home hasn't even put the grave marker at the burial site yet.* The only assurance she had they were even at Gordon's gravesite was they were next to Grandma Jo's grave marker. Brad later explained the grave marker wouldn't be placed at the site for months, allowing the ground to settle. Still, Annie struggled to relinquish her impression the funeral home director was really a villain who tied beautiful women to train tracks. *No wonder he runs a funeral home, and no wonder his building sits next to the train tracks running through town.*

The preacher from the church where Grandma Jo got married, although not the one who officiated at her ceremony, performed a small graveside service for Gordon. Mother, Brad and Annie were the only ones in attendance. By then, the elation Annie felt at the hospital thinking Gordon was with God was replaced by a sense of loss. She shed tears along with Mother and Brad, who pretended he wasn't crying but rather struggling with a nasty cough. The service was short, ending in the song "Amazing Grace." The four of them started out strong, but after the first two lines, it was only the preacher who sang. No one else knew the words.

While the ground at the grave site settled, Annie convinced Mother to use some of the money from Gordon's disability check from the government, which arrived in the mail soon after his death, to add a plate to Gordon's grave marker that read:

Son, brother, uncle, artist

When visiting the cemetery and looking at the new gravestone and shiny metal plate, Annie remembered the feeling she had had in the hospital that Gordon was still with her, just in a different form. Of course it wasn't the form she preferred. She much more wanted to sit with him at the dock where they worked on their art together. *But then who am I to want him to come back to the physical form?* She wasn't able to re-experience the happiness she felt in the hospital, but she did have the memory, which allowed her to continue to believe.

•••

Annie continued sleeping on her mattress in Mother's bedroom instead of reclaiming the second bedroom. Mother offered to help her take apart the bed and move the frame and mattress into the living room until Linda and Gary came to retrieve the set, but Annie refused. Her life had changed so much over the past two months. She'd reassigned value to the things she once felt were important, like having her own bedroom and having the freedom to go where she wanted and do what she pleased without having someone dependent on her for care.

It all began with moving my mattress out of my bedroom. I don't want the parts of my life Gordon changed to go away when I move my mattress back, she thought as she sat on the couch waiting for Linda and Gary to arrive. Her legs were crossed, both feet twitching, as she waited for their knock at the door. Out of habit, she still checked her watch to see if it was time for Gordon's next bathroom break. She sighed and rose from the couch to pour Linda a glass of diet pop. When Annie opened the door to Linda's quick little knocks, she smiled and held out the diet pop for Linda to take.

"Oh, honey, I'm so sorry for your loss," Linda said, pushing the door open and embracing Annie in a hug. Annie wrapped her free arm around Linda and held up the glass with the other to keep from spilling it. Gary squeezed by them and disappeared into Gordon's room. Upon releasing her, Linda took the diet pop from Annie's hand and led her to the couch. They both sat down, and Linda tried to comfort Annie. *She knew how hard it was at the beginning. Yet she doesn't doubt I miss him and loved him.*

To keep from crying, Annie thought about one of her favorite Gordon memories. She only wished she'd been there to see it…him throwing a cup of diet pop at Linda.

•••

Annie returned to her position as a cashier at the grocery store. As Louise promised, Annie kept her seniority and returned to the schedule she was working before her summer off. On her first day back, as she crossed the bridge over the train tracks, Annie realized she'd never re-set the minute hand on her watch to match the clock at the store. She wondered whether Cody would let her tardiness slide, especially after their talk that night at his house. But when she reached the edge of the parking lot, she saw him standing by her register with his arms crossed in front of his chest. Walking in the door, before Cody could say anything, Annie protested, "I'm only a minute late." She tried to hide she was out of breath. She whipped her smock out from under the register and slipped it over her head.

"Then it's only a minute you'll have to stay late to work a full eight hours," he snapped. He rolled his eyes and glared at her.

She met his gaze and mouthed, "You're such a prick."

"Thank you," he replied, raising one of his eyebrows.

Annie had to turn her head to hide her smile.

•••

Annie was sitting at the chess table down at the dock when she wrote the words to Cody's song. The soft wind from the bright blue sky carried the words down to her. They came just in time, as Cody was leaving for college the following week. They worked together after the store closed and into the early morning hours to fit the words to the melody. Neither spoke about what the song meant, but they both knew the song spoke to them the same. The song began about the fear of the unknown accompanying death and haunting those still living. The song's ending, however, was about the faith in life continuing, though in a different form, which replaces fear and eases pain, although never eliminating the feeling of loss.

They worked on the song in Cody's basement, comfortably decorated with well used furniture, a couch cushion with a tear in it and the television case held together with duct tape. Annie sat across from him at the table, as he played his guitar into a microphone, making the first recording of the song. Listening to the music, Annie's heart was warmed knowing Cody chose to allow her, one of the Everyone Elses, to see him in this third world he lived in. They made three copies of the song, one for Cody, one for Annie, and one for Ms. Erwin. When Annie wasn't able to come up with a favor before Cody left for school, she said she'd get back to him over Christmas break.

•••

In time, Annie began to think of Gordon less and less, though she was always aware he'd helped her to become a better person. By the middle of the fall semester of her junior year, Annie found herself preoccupied with issues that demanded her attention and wouldn't let her continue living in the past. For instance, she had to learn how to put up with the squirrelly new manager who took Cody's place at work. Not to mention Ms. Erwin took delight in assigning her honors English class an average of one hour of homework every night!

When Kelly caught Annie's attention in the hall between classes and started talking to her one morning, it took Annie a moment to understand what Kelly was talking about.

"How is he?" Kelly had asked.

"Who?"

"Your uncle!" Kelly exclaimed.

"Oh," Annie said, surprised at how much her life had already changed since the summer. "He passed away this summer."

"I'm sorry," Kelly said, looking as if she truly were sorry. "I wondered if something had happened to him when I didn't see you out walking with him anymore. Were you able to teach him about Jesus?" She shifted her books in her arms and looked eagerly at Annie.

Annie smiled, "Let's just say I'm positive he's with God."

Kelly smiled and reached out to touch Annie's shoulder. "Well, I hope you and your mom are okay. I hope you don't mind that I bothered you at school."

Annie's eyes widened. *Why would she say a thing like that?* Then the sick feeling of hypocrisy came over Annie. *What if I'd been wrong our freshman year? What if Kelly hadn't seen me and ignored me? What if all this time she thought I was the one who made the rule not to talk at school?* Kelly continued walking to her next period class. Annie called out after her, "Hey, Kelly?"

Kelly paused and turned around.

"You didn't bother me. You can talk to me any time."

Kelly smiled and nodded. "See ya at lunch, then!" she called from down the hall.

"Yeah, see ya at lunch," Annie replied.

•••

Even though Annie hadn't celebrated Christmas with Gordon (going to the store to buy a box of shirts and to the post office to mail them didn't count), she found herself missing him on Christmas Eve when she exchanged presents with Mother and Brad. Feeling the warmth of the space heater Brad had brought them, they sat in the living room eating pieces of pie with their opened gifts spread out around them. Annie and Mother were eating pumpkin pie, while Brad was eating a piece of apple. He shifted the conversation to Gordon.

"So, I always wondered how it was having him live with you."

"Fine," Annie said, taking a bite of whipped cream.

"What'd you do with him all day?" Brad asked Mother.

Mother shook her head and swallowed her bite of pie. "Annie was the one who cared for him."

Brad looked at Annie and raised his eyebrows to ask her the same question.

Annie swallowed another bite of pie. "He slept a lot and colored."

"Colored? Like when he was a kid?"

Mother nodded. Annie put her plate on the coffee table and walked into her bedroom. She went to the pile of Gordon's belongings she'd stored in the closet and pulled out the pictures Gordon had colored. On the top of the pile was the unfinished one with wavy lines he'd started in the hospital. She removed it from the pile and put it back into the closet. She then took the rest of the papers into the living room to show Brad. Mother leaned over to look at them as Brad shuffled through the pile.

"You kept these?" Mother asked Annie.

"Obviously," Brad replied, rolling his eyes. Mother punched him on the arm.

"I never understood how he could be so happy just coloring circles over and over," Brad said. He handed the pile of pictures back to Annie, who began to look through them. "What are you going to do with those?" he asked.

"Frame my favorite," she replied.

•••

The favor Annie requested as payment for writing the words to Cody's song was for him to give her two trips into the city over his Christmas break. The first trip took place at the beginning so Annie could drop off Gordon's picture at the downtown framing gallery. The second trip took place near the end of his break so she could pick up the finished product. When the framer unwrapped the brown paper from around the picture, Annie was happy she hadn't let herself be talked into cutting the edges of the pictures so they could use a less expensive, already assembled frame. The picture was beautiful in its shiny black frame. It looked like a piece of artwork belonging in a museum.

After she sat back down in the front seat of Cody's small blue rusty car, having placed her picture in the back seat, Cody said, "I was wondering if you wanted to do something." He coughed and looked out the front window. "We could see a movie or go to dinner…but that seems kind of lame."

Annie smiled at his nervousness. It was cute. She thought for a minute. "Do you like piano music?"

"Sure."

"Do you mind the cold?"

"No," he shrugged.

Looking at her watch, she said, "I know someone giving a free concert at a church right about now if you want to go."

"Lead the way," Cody said, putting the car in gear.